UNDEAD

LIVING

EDITED BY

THOMAS M. MALAFARINA

UNDEAD LIVING

FIRST SUNBURY PRESS EDITION
Printed in the United States of America
October 2013

Trade Paperback ISBN: 978-1-62006-285-2
Mobipocket format (Kindle) ISBN: 978-1-62006-286-9
ePub format (Nook) ISBN: 978-1-62006-287-6

Published by:
Sunbury Press
Mechanicsburg, PA
www.sunburypress.com

Mechanicsburg, Pennsylvania   USA

TABLE OF CONTENTS

FOREWORD

In late April of 2013 I was approached by my publisher, Lawrence Knorr of Sunbury Press, and asked to assume the role of editor and curator for Sunbury Press's first ever assorted horror short story anthology. I was also asked to write this foreword and a short story for the book as well. I was thrilled with the opportunity, and although I was working on a new novel as well as a number of short stories, I jumped at the chance. You see, I seldom have much time to read other writers' works (unless they are in audio book format), so for me the anthology meant forcing myself to do so.

The idea of the anthology was to put out an open request for submissions based on the general theme "Contemporary Undead," and was to include, zombies, ghosts, vampires, or other such undead creatures and see what sort of entries we might receive. I was truly not expecting to receive very many entries, since this was our first foray into such a project, and I most certainly had not expected to receive any from outside of the United States. However, I was pleasantly surprised to discover that within three weeks of setting up the submission website, we had already received five entries, including some from Sweden and Italy. After about nine submissions, things slowed down for a while. Then we eventually got another wave of stories, and the real fun began. Some of the stories are quite frightening, some over the top gory, and some just a bit bizarre.

Despite my previously mentioned busy schedule, I was happy to take the time to read each and every one of them. As curator, it was my job to pick which stories would become part of the anthology and which we would pass on. Having my own collection of rejection letters, I know first hand what it feels like to be passed over for inclusion, and I still get rejected more often than I care to mention.

For those authors whose stories were chosen, congratulations, thank-you, and welcome to this collection. For those of you who were not; please, by all means keep writing, keep submitting, and best of luck submitting your stories to other markets where they might be a better fit.

All of the stories were good, but not all of the stories were a good match for what I had in mind for this anthology. Such is life. As I said, it happens to all of us, and I honestly feel your pain.

I hope you readers enjoy this collection of contemporary undead tales and wish you many pleasant dreams (he said with tongue firmly planted in cheek) in the nights ahead.

THOMAS M. MALAFARINA
SEPTEMBER 2013

FEEDING FRENZY

by Michael Collins

Michael Collins received a B.A. in Dramatic Writing
from the University of Michigan and an M.A. in
Creative Writing from Boston University. His ten-
minute play, *The Playground*, was produced at the
Calderwood Pavilion in 2005 and received a
favorable review from *The Boston Herald*. His book
of short stories, *Fenwyck Bumblerut's Backyard
Biographies*, was published by Halcyon press in
2012.

Fear of sunlight is a myth. So is hatred of garlic. And
the scalding touch of the cross. Overstreet wore a silver
chain around his neck, and two overlaid nails formed the
pendant. Jesus died on the cross, nailed on wooden
planks, suffering for the sins of Mankind, enduring
excruciating agony, ignominy, death.

Overstreet was a man of darkness, but he lived in the
light of day, in the mist of twilight, and the black hole of
night. There were hundreds like him, born in the shadows,
living secret lives, paying homage to an idol bathed in the
blood of men.

The sanctity of blood purifies me.

***

The Sam Browne gun belt snapped into place around
his waist. A silver badge gleamed in the half-light of his
bedroom, and the fan blades spun in slow-motion. The
Smith and Wesson M&P polymer-framed pistol clicked into
the triple-retention Safariland holster. The baby-blue
patrolman's shirt heightened the dull gray pallor of his
skin. Overstreet looked like a porcelain statue, a marble
effigy with veiny arms and jet black hair. He studied his
reflection in the mirror: the sagging flesh, the fire-red eyes,
starved veins and capillaries ready to implode. He was

thirsty, ravenous, and bursting at the seams to break out of his shell.

The sanctity of blood purifies me.

He moved down the dark hallway. Wooden slats creaked under the rubber soles of his Magnum Stealth Force boots. The front door eased shut behind him, and he walked out into the night. One thought consumed him. One thought dominated every fiber of his being, every second of his existence.

The feeding frenzy...

***

"Are you ready to DIE-DIE-DIE!"

A throw-back punk rock band belted out lyrics under the cover of an electric guitar. Overstreet cut the radio down and glanced at the man in the passenger seat. Johnnie Hartman was dead to the world. He reeked of booze, stale cigarettes, and cheap perfume. He had a wife. But he also had plenty of women on the side. The lipstick on his lapel was a dead give-away. The radio crackled and hissed. The Dispatcher's voice broke the silence.

"Fifteen-E-Twenty-Six-Nights?"

Overstreet picked up the handheld and keyed-up with his thumb.

"Twenty-Six, go ahead."

"Twenty-Six, I need to show you en route to a code-three Disturbance/No Injuries at ninety-six-oh-one Marlive Lane. An intoxicated male is throwing rocks at the caller's window."

"That's negative. Hold me out on a Directed Patrol Assignment at one-thousand-one South Loop West, authority Sergeant Simmons of Watch Command."

Overstreet slid the mike into its dashboard cradle, placed both hands firmly on the wheel, and looked out at the empty roadway. Flickering street lamps flashed by, a three-legged dog hobbled down the street, and a homeless man urinated in a storm drain.

"You're full of surprises, rookie."

Overstreet glanced over his right shoulder. Johnnie Hartman was awake, head tilted back, sucking at the spout of a silver flask, whiskey spilling down his chin. His carotid artery pulsed with life.

4

"You look dead to the world," Overstreet said as his eyes returned to the shadows of the city streets.

"I am dead. Night shift has sucked the life out of me. Only the booze keeps me goin'."

"Maybe, you shouldn't have pissed down Captain Miller's throat like that. You'd still be on day shift with weekends off."

"Captain Miller's a fairy, and so are you, rookie. So are you."

Johnnie threw his head back and swallowed more whiskey. Overstreet focused on the road. Half-remembered apparitions floated in on a tide of memory. A swirling red whirlpool sucked him down, down, down into the abyss. He remembered his first kill: the fear of the hunted, the triumph of the predator, the blood coursing through his veins, filling his body with strength. Overstreet gripped the steering wheel so tight that the plastic cracked. Static hissed out of the radio, and the engine revved up to about five-thousand rotations-per-minute. The street lamps flickered and went out. Pitch-black darkness closed in around them. BEEP-BEEP-BEEP-BEEP. Johnnie's Timex went berserk.

"Damn alarm won't turn off," he said, fumbling with the buttons.

BEEP-BEEP-BEEP-BEEP. Johnny slammed his wrist against the dashboard, and the cheap plastic face erupted in a spiderweb of cracks.

"Cheap piece of shit. Next time I'll buy a Casio."

Overstreet cut the wheel left, pulling into the alley behind Tweety's Diamond Inn Motel. He could taste blood in the back of his throat: a coarse, metallic tinge. He ran his tongue over his teeth, appraising the contours of the molars, canines, and incisors. He nicked the tip of his tongue on a razor-sharp enamel edge, but the cut was dry. No blood. Overstreet's eyes glowed red.

"Where the hell are we? I thought we were s'posed to be on Directed Patrol at Main and The Loop."

"It's a surprise. Don't you like surprises?"

"I hate surprises."

"I rented you a room."

"You *what*?"

5

"I rented you a room at Tweety's."

"That's a crack-motel. Nothin' but crack-whores, crack-rock, and crack-pipes."

"I got you a girl, too."

Johnnie frowned, fiddling with the wedding band on the ring finger of his left hand. Overstreet smiled, and a pair of canines poked down like arrowheads over the edge of his lower lip. But it was too dark for Johnnie to see.

"Why are you doin' this for me?"

"Tomorrow's my last day on the rookie baby-sitting program. I thought I'd give you a going-away-present. A little thank-you for all the time you've spent training me up."

Overstreet held up a dull brass key. Johnnie sat and stared. Then he smiled.

"You're okay, rook. You're okay by me."

"Room forty two. Take your time. Enjoy yourself. I'll be waiting here when you get done."

The passenger door slammed shut, and Johnnie Hartman receded into the darkness. Overstreet's eyes glowed red. A single thought consumed him.

Feeding frenzy...

***

A little bell jingled as the office door swung open. A man with a greasy comb-over and bags under his eyes sat behind a layer of protective glass. He leaned back in a swivel chair behind his desk. A prostitute named Jersey sat in a molded plastic seat against the wall, smearing a blob of lipstick across her face. A cop stepped into the office. Jersey looked up, but she didn't have time to scream. Overstreet punched her in the mouth, knocking out most of her teeth. He wrapped his fingers in her hair, jerked her chin back, and sunk his canines into her throat.

The manager stood up on shaky legs, and his chair toppled over backwards. His greasy comb-over flopped to one side. His eyes wide, he tried to scream, but no sound came out. Jersey twitched a little in her chair as the cop gorged on her neck like a tick.

"Oh my god-oh my god-oh my god-oh my god..." the manager said, reaching for the phone.

Overstreet looked up, his eyes red, his gray face flecked with blood. He dropped the limp body onto the linoleum. Then he moved forward, his heels clicking across the laminate tile.

"9-1-1, what's your emergency?"

"HELP ME!"

Overstreet's fist slammed through the glass. Razor-sharp slivers zinged through the air like missiles. He clenched a fistful of fabric and wrenched the manager head-first through the plate-glass window.

"No! Please! Jesus, please!"

Overstreet ripped out the man's trachea. As he drank the geyser of blood, life coursed through his veins. One thought consumed him:

Feeding frenzy...

***

His cell phone rang. Johnnie Hartman reached down and fumbled around in the front pocket of the slacks that were balled-up on the carpet beside the bed. He caught the call on the fourth ring.

"Becky, I'm workin'. What the hell do you want?"

No answer. Just crying on the other end.

"What's the matter with you?" Johnnie asked, his voice rising.

No answer. Just crying.

"Quit cryin', dammit!"

Johnnie killed the call and tossed the phone on the bedside table. He looked over at the woman next to him. She had bags under her eyes, dyed red hair, and an open sore on her left cheek.

"All Becky does is cry. Night and day. Waa-waa-waa. All day long."

The woman on the bed didn't answer. She didn't even move.

"Becky's my wife."

Still no answer. Johnnie thought about it for a minute.

"Ready for round-two?"

The woman killed the TV. and turned to face him.

***

Overstreet opened his eyes. He stared down at the blood-trail. The office looked like a slaughter house. Bodies

7

lay on the floor, carcasses on the cold, hard tile. Hand-prints, palm-prints, foot-prints stamped in blood across the walls. Overstreet glanced at the counter. He reached through the hole in the glass and picked up the guest register. There were only two occupied rooms.

***

Mark Thomas popped a zit in front of the bathroom mirror. He grimaced and studied his reflection. Fifty years old with a bowling-ball gut and flabby arms, Mark hated life almost as much as he hated his wife of thirty plus years. A couple times a month, he just had to get away from it all: the wife, the kids, the dog, the house with the pretty picket fence. He had to leave it all behind him and enjoy a little quality time at Tweety's Diamond Inn with Jersey, his special friend, his ace in the hole, his girl on the side. Mark turned the knob, and water coursed through the rusty pipes. He picked up his toothbrush.

There was a knock on the front door. He shut the water off. Jersey had left ten minutes ago for a pack of cigarettes. He hadn't expected her back so soon. There was another knock.

"Use your key!" Mark shouted from the bathroom, his mouth full of paste.

There was a moment of silence. Then another knock. Grumbling, Mark wrapped a towel around his waist and plodded heavily across the carpet. He put his eye to the peep-hole. A dark outline materialized on the other side of the door.

"Who is it?"

"Police. Open up."

"I didn't call the police."

Overstreet kicked in the door. Mark sprawled back across the carpet, his eyes wide, his lower lip split. The cop stood in the shadows of the doorway.

"Are you crazy? You just busted my door down!"

"Sorry."

"Who the hell do you think you are? Do you have a warrant?"

"No."

"I'll have your job! I'll have your badge! I'll –"

8

Bathed in blood, Overstreet stepped forward into the light. A sharp intake of breath, a gasp, sounded as Mark Thomas put his hand to his mouth. Overstreet moved into the room, his canines glistening.

***

As Johnnie Hartman pulled up his pants, he looked at the door. He'd heard something. *Thunder, maybe? No, it sounded more like a scream.* The toilet flushed. Mandy stumbled out of the bathroom, scratching her leg.

"Ready for round-three, Officer?"

"Not tonight, sweetheart. I got some calls to run."

"So you're through with me?"

"Yeah, I'm through with you, babe."

"Good. I'm beat,but your partner paid me real well to show you a good time."

"Mission accomplished, Mandy. I had a helluva time."

"Tell your wife I said 'hi'."

"You got it, babe," Johnnie said, strapping on his gun belt.

Mandy grabbed her Newports off of the bedside table and headed for the door. Lighting a cigarette, she walked out of the room. Johnny looked at his reflection in the bathroom mirror. His face was a wreck: hollowed-out eyes, puffy red cheeks. He looked like a blow fish ready to pop. He pulled out his silver flask and took a chug of whiskey. He came up for air. Then he took another swig.

A high-pitched scream shattered the silence. Johnnie coughed, spraying liquor all over the carpet. He turned to face the open door. Another scream, more faint this time, but somehow more desperate. Then came the sound of rending flesh. Growling, tearing, moaning. Then silence. *A dog fight, maybe. Gotta be a dog fight.* Johnnie faced the door. Sweat streamed into his eyes. His heart beat like a jackhammer in his chest. He sensed death in the air, the ebbing of life, the onset of decay. Then he heard footsteps echo down the hallway. Footfalls on a slab of concrete. Drawing close, closer. A figure stood in the shadows of the open doorway. A mere silhouette. A man stepped into the light. Not a man. A monster.

"Hey, Johnnie."

Overstreet flung a bloody scalp on the carpet. Johnnie stumbled back, hand over his mouth, dry-heaving, retching in the corner.

"Are you ready to die?"

"What is this?" Johnnie asked, doubled-over in the corner, his face green.

"This is a feeding frenzy."

Johnnie just looked at him, his face blank.

"Who are you?"

"I'm your partner. Well, *ex*-partner, really."

"Why are you doin' this?"

"Because it's what I do."

Then Johnnie experienced a moment of clarity. He saw the truth.

"You're not a man. What the hell are you?"

Overstreet laughed.

"I'm that monster in all those fairy tales. The guy with the long black cloak in a stone castle out there in Romania or wherever the hell else."

Johnnie looked down at the bloody strip of flesh; clumps of hair splayed-out across the carpet.

"You butchered that woman."

"Yeah, I did."

"You...you killed that...that whore."

"I kill a lotta people. And guess what?"

"What?"

"I'm gonna kill you, too."

Overstreet moved into the room. Johnnie stumbled back, pulled his pistol, and fired one, two, three times. He kept pulling the trigger until the firing pin clicked on an empty chamber. Overstreet bucked a little each time a red-hot round pounded through his flesh. He pounced like a wolf, driving for the carotid artery, rending flesh, muscle, and bone. Johnnie screamed. Blood spurted the walls, pooled on the carpet, ran down his shirt, and dyed the gleaming silver badge red. The vampire gorged until he was full.

***

A man dressed in an Armani suit walked out of room forty two. He stepped over the body on the landing and continued down the stairs. The parking lot was almost

10

empty. Sirens wailed in the distance. The man walked up to a silver Mercedes, which was parked in the middle of the lot. He clicked the keyless entry remote, climbed into the driver seat, and turned the key in the ignition. Thick black smoke rolled over the rooftop. The man glanced at his gold Rolex Ambassador. Two-thirty five.

Good. I'll just make my next appointment.

Overstreet peeled-out down the street as flames engulfed Tweety's Diamond Inn.

THE SUPREME RACE

by Catherine Jordan

Catherine Jordan is a Pennsylvania author who enjoys writing in different genres. She strives to put down thought-provoking, consequential stories. Ms. Jordan lives in central PA and is a wife and mother of five children. She has been writing stories since learning to hold a pencil.

Her debut horror novel, *Seeking Samiel*, is intended to be a series, and she is working on the sequel. Her work has been published in a variety of on-line publications and she has a short story, *The Green Eyed Monster*, in an anthology, *A Community of Writers*, edited by Ann Elia Stewart.

Their enemy lies on his bed, asleep in his cold house. They have been watching him for years. His room is dark, but they can see inside quite well. The clock on his bedside table reads 2:43 a.m. The small town where he lives is quiet during the winter. Neighboring houses are far apart. As far as his family and friends will know, he will have simply disappeared. They will leave no trace behind.

The enemy twitches in his sleep, and Labal leans in, poised to lunge, but Labal realizes the twitch was a shiver, because his breath is forming clouds above his open mouth every time he exhales. Labal observes Alastor, who is under the bed, having crawled there a few hours ago. Labal stands silently by the bedside. The Masses huddle in the corner behind the door with fists clenched, ready to fight. They shove each other where they have gathered, restless. The Masses are hungry.

The Masses are brute muscle and are brought along only when necessary. Sometimes they cajole or bully, but otherwise, their brains are useless. Their heads droop to their necks, and their tongues loll out of their mouths. They will not attack without a strict order from an Intellect.

The enemy's dog, Rex—a burly, dark haired standard poodle, points its snout around the room. Labal approves of the enemy's choice of guard dog. Standard poodles, especially this one, are large and can be trained to be aggressive. The breed is a hunting dog, a pointer. But, since Labal's black flesh is concealed in the bedroom's vapid darkness, the dog questions Labal and his company's presence.

Still, Rex smells intruders. What can the dog make out of them? The animal can't possibly count their numbers amongst his master, but probably senses there are many. The thing does not understand motive, only intent. Rex leaves the room, whimpering into the dimly lit hall. Best the dog leave, so they won't have to include him in their imminent carnage.

Their quest against the enemy and his kind is not a nebulous disdain; their hatred is not a general attitude. Sides have been drawn and are known. Labal's side knows only destruction and decay. Life no longer has any meaning for Labal, although he recognizes that it did once upon a time. Desire, discovery, love—he considers these things mythological, and they no longer propel him. Only destruction and decay do.

They had been assigned to the enemy at the moment of his conception, for it was foretold that this one would make the discovery that will bring about their end. Labal and Alastor watched and walked with him, unseen. They sifted though his trash and read everything he read, analyzed everything he said and heard, and saw all he saw. Why they were not permitted to take the enemy sooner, before the discovery was made, was never revealed to Labal.

There was no known antidote for the potent neurotoxin, tetrodotoxin—essentially a nerve blocker, which puts their kind in what appears to be a coma-like state—until last week, when the enemy discovered the antidote. The rest of the world does not yet know that the antidote exists or that one half milligram in a sip, injection, or pill will "cure".

Tetrodotoxin is part of their DNA. It is what makes them who they are. Scientists refer to them as catatonic schizophrenics. Most humans call them zombies. Zombies call themselves the supreme race, and they do not want to be "cured". Even The Masses, who have slightly elevated levels of tetrodotoxin (thus the drooped necks, open mouths, and general uselessness), understand that the so-called "cure" will bring their demise.

Labal had witnessed a clinical trial. An Intellect had been caged and strapped to a metal chair, which was bolted into a cement floor in the lab where the enemy worked as a scientist. No human wanted any direct contact with a zombie, and so as soon as the enemy pushed the button on the wall outside the cage, a pre-filled syringe attached to a mechanized arm swung through the bars and into The Intellect's arm.

There was no cure. The Intellect did not revert to his human state, free from rot. His body tensed, and a second later, he collapsed.

The enemy left The Intellect strapped to the chair for days, to observe. All he observed was an unanimated form. The Intellect did not rise again from the dead. He did not decay any faster or decompose into a pile of ashes. Well, not until he was unstrapped and thrown into the incinerator.

That was when Labal wanted to burst through the vent where he hid and strap the enemy to the bolted chair where he would watch Labal smash every syringe. Afterward, Labal would eat him alive. Labal would start with his feet. Then his hands. Arms. Legs. He would pull out muscles, gnaw on bones, and suck out marrow while the appendage was still attached. Then Labal would eviscerate him, eating his intestines inch by inch, his organs piece by piece.

However, Labal has been ordered not to consume the enemy. He is to infect him with tetrodotoxin through a single bite. Their toxin will eat him from the inside out. Then the enemy will be like them and he will no longer be the enemy.

The enemy had worked tirelessly for years to discover the antidote. Since the discovery, the enemy considers his job complete and has fallen fast asleep. They know he sleeps with a gun and that he hid syringes of the antidote under his pillow, just in case

What the enemy failed to realize is that he won't want to inject himself after he is infected; the toxin works that fast on both the body and the mind. As for the gun, it is of no concern to them.

From the hall, Labal hears oncoming footsteps. There is trepidation in the footsteps, and they stop outside the bedroom door. Labal smells sickly sweet cologne from the powders, shampoos, and lotions that fragrance a female's body. A woman enters behind Labal, sniffing and wrapping her arms around herself. She wrinkles her nose, no doubt smelling the rot, sulfur, and acrid earth that perfume Labal and those with him. They have not yet taken shape in her eyes, and like the dog, she perceives something is in the room but can't see. Labal senses fear rising in her.

Her small hand feels along the wall for the light switch.

Light floods the enemy's bedroom. Labal hisses and Alastor squirms farther under the bed. The Masses in the corner knot together, their backs to the light. Labal, however, keeps his eyes wide open, braving the light's fire.

Labal swipes at her, his fingernails raking her cheek. Blood runs thick, for the cut is deep. Labal has cut throats and dismembered appendages with his nails. He has sliced off large chunks of flesh, and several times has ripped away half a face with his nails.

She opens her mouth to scream and Labal leaps on her, clamping his hand over her mouth. He forces her to the floor and presses his weight upon her to squash her dismal struggle. Both hands cover her nose and mouth, his elbows stretched out to pin her shoulders. Her bare feet thud against the carpeted floor.

Labal turns toward the bed. Alastor remains in place, and the enemy is still asleep.

Her tongue laps against Labal's hand and he feels the tips of her teeth graze his palms. "I am something you do not want to taste," he whispers in her ear. Suffocation is slow—Labal thoroughly enjoys the process—and he won't loosen his grip. The expression on her face changes from fear to pleading.

15

Her lids slowly close and she stops struggling. After another minute, her limbs jerk once, then twice in convulsion. Her lids snap open, the whites of her eyes hemorrhaging and turning a deep pink. Then her eyes drift to the left and they close forever. Labal lifts her wrist and licks it. He wants to take a bite, but she is not on the menu.

Death is what they do. Some would say that death—the walking dead—is what they create. It only takes one bite to infect a human with their toxin. Any defense is futile. The power behind the fist is not important. A sharp blade will fold like foil. Guns are useless, even if the shot is accurate. It doesn't matter how fast you can run. They will get you. One bite propagates their species.

Labal climbs off the woman and dashes toward the wall, flipping off the light. There is a moment of shuffling as Alastor and the ones in the corner regain their composure.

"Is she dead?" Alastor asks.

"Quite," Labal says.

"Did you bite her?" Alastor asks.

"No. She will stay dead."

"Bite her!" came a scream from The Masses.

The enemy awakens. Though it is dark, the night isn't thick enough to cloud them from him. He is already used to the lighting, or lack of it, and his eyes grow wider as his stare moves from Labal to The Masses. He sits up and snakes a hand under his pillow, but he finds nothing. The look of surprise on his face is delicious. Alastor has the syringes under the bed. The enemy was so sound asleep that Alastor's hand slid under the enemy's pillow without disturbing him.

Under the bed, Alastor squirms out toward the edge ready to scoop up the enemy's dangling feet. Labal crouches to pounce on his back. Labal looks to The Masses to be sure they are ready in case he runs passed him. Labal's teeth and saliva will pass the tetrodotoxin into his blood stream. It has to be done. This is about survival.

After the enemy becomes one of them, he will destroy the antidote by his own volition. So it has been foretold.

16

The enemy throws off the covers and hops off the bed. He wears jeans and a white t-shirt. Gritting his decaying teeth, Alastor swings out both arms and grasps him by his ankles. The enemy falls with a thump to the floor, but is quickly back on his feet. He pulls out the handgun.

He aims his gun at Labal's heart and pulls the trigger. Labal hears a pop and a dull thwack as the bullet enters his already collapsed chest. A thin stream of smoke wisps out of the hole, but nothing else.

"You can't kill what's already dead," Labal says with a sneer.

Guns have been effective in intimidating The Masses, but not The Intellects. Humans can't seem to tell The Masses from the Intellects, at least not when faced with only a moment's notice for defense. Labal smiles at the gun. He understands and can sympathize with the notion of a last-ditch-effort.

Labal lunges forward and grasps the enemy in a great bear hug, pinning his arms at his sides, the gun falling to the floor.

The enemy squirms. He grunts and kicks. His face takes on a ghastly white as the color drains.

"You are like a little bug," Labal says. "Annoying. I could release you and watch you scurry for my own amusement before squashing you. Look at the ones in the corner. Their hunger is never satisfied."

Labal is eye to eye with the enemy, looking deep into watery eyes that dart back and forth from The Masses to Labal's eyes to Labal's mouth. Labal considers the enemy quite disgusting, all white skinned and fleshy and unmarked. His brown eyes possess a life-like quality that causes Labal to raise what is left of his rotting lip in revulsion.

"No, please. No. I can save you all," the enemy whimpers. "I, I can release you from..."

"You would inject your antidote—your poison—into our arms, murdering us by the millions!" Labal screams.

Holding the enemy tight in one burly arm, Labal snatches the enemy's hand and brings it to his lips. "The wrist," he says, affirming his decision to avoid the neck, an area The Masses always go for at first bite.

Alastor slithers out from under the bed. He tilts his head and furrows his already crooked eyebrows at Labal. "Why the wrist?"

"I don't want a gash in his throat. If I go for the wrist, the mark won't be as noticeable. He has to come with us to destroy the antidote. We don't want any suspicion."

Alastor gives a half nod of agreement.

Labal gazes upon the enemy's flesh, thinking how easy and tempting it is to stuff the entire hand into his watering maw. The artery throbs under white skin. Labal laps at the tendon, sliding it between his snaggle teeth, snapping the tendon right through the skin.

The enemy's scream cuts through the night's silence like a razor. Blood streams out and splatters into Labal's mouth and down his chin. Since his jaw is loose, he clamps down on the wrist and sucks at the warm flow. The enemy's moan fills his ears and he listens closely for the breathing to slow. Labal feels the heartbeat weaken, and each burst of blood becomes more sluggish than the previous one, dwindling to a trickle.

"He is hanging onto life. It is time," Labal says to Alastor.

Labal drops the enemy to the floor and pries open and holds the enemy's mouth wide as he retches a torrent of blood back into the enemy's mouth. As long as some of the hot, black liquid is swallowed, that would be enough.

Labal releases him.

The enemy lays quietly for a moment or two before he coughs. He coughs again and moans faintly, as if awakening from a disturbed sleep. With a great gasp, he suddenly sits up like a marionette jerked to animated life. His breathing quickens, he blinks and blinks as the irises lose their brown, taking on the distinct, lifeless blue-gray color. His skin washes into a pale, sickly hue.

"There," Labal says to him. "That wasn't so bad, was it?"

He looks down at his blood drenched t-shirt. Titling his head to look behind Labal, Labal realizes he is just now noticing the woman on the floor.

"She's dead," Labal says.

"She was my wife," he says. He shrugs.

Labal always found the visible change in the body fascinating, but even more interesting was the change he couldn't see, the change in the brain. Acceptance, acquiescence, morbid passivity. It was as if a flip had been switched, and oh, how Labal wished he could watch the brain shrivel, as he figured it must, and morph into a viable, functioning intelligence.

Labal had not reduced him to one of those things lurking in the corner. It all has to do with the transformation: If Labal were to only take a bite, the enemy would become one of The Masses; if blood is shared, well, then, Intellect begets Intellect. Conversion through blood sharing is a privilege reserved for the chosen few.

"Now," Labal says as he pulls him to his feet. "Let's go hose you down and then destroy that antidote."

"I've been a fool," he says with remorse in his voice.

"All men are fools," Labal says. He straightens his shoulders. "But now you are one of us, the walking dead. Welcome to your new race."

Labal addresses The Masses. "It is time for the main attack."

The newly converted one watches The Masses climb out the window. They are to clamor through town and bite into everyone they see as they make their way to the research lab. The lab will be smashed and then burned, the antidote destroyed. Whatever humans are left alive will be kept and bred like cows and sheep.

"The war continues," says Alastor.

"And the Intellects will rule," Labal says. "We are the supreme race."

THE STORM

by Kristina R. Mosley

Kristina R. Mosley lives in Kensett, Arkansas. Her work has been featured in numerous publications, including *Scifaikuest*, *Tales from the Grave*, *Eschatology*, *Micro Horror*, and *The Old Weird South*. She has a languishing writing block, but she tweets too often at twitter.com/elstupacabra.

Emma sat on her bed reading a book. A strong wind blew outside, and the beams in the ceiling groaned. Her border collie, Mac, who lay at the foot of the bed, lifted his head and whined.

"It's just the wind, boy," she said nervously. A rock flew into the window by her head, cracking the glass in a spider web pattern. She yelped. A ghostly wailing cut through the moaning outside. Mac jumped off the bed and howled.

Her mother burst into the room, her red hair in a ponytail and light blue paint dotting her t-shirt and jeans. "There's a tornado. We have to get out of here."

Emma tossed her book on the bed. Her rag doll bounced with the impact. Some of the doll's yellow yarn hair had fallen out over the years, and its pink and purple dress had faded with age. She reached for the doll but stopped. I'm twelve, she thought. I'm too old for dolls. The toy's green, painted-on eyes stared at the girl, like it was waiting for an answer.

"Hurry, Emma," her mother said.

"Okay." She left the doll in its place by the windowsill and ran after her mother. Her long brown hair swished back and forth behind her. Mac followed.

They passed Emma's sister Julie's room, unused since the family inherited the farm two months earlier. Julie stays away because she didn't want to move, Emma thought.

"Kate, Emma, we have to get to the storm cellar," Emma's dad called from the first floor.

"Yes, dear." Kate replied. She and her daughter ran down the stairs and found the brown-haired man waiting. His clothes were speckled blue from repainting the kitchen.

I wanted to help, Emma thought, but they said I was too small.

"Why are you waiting, George?" Her mother's voice brought the girl out of her thoughts.

"I didn't want to leave you too far behind. Let's go."

The family ran outside, the tornado siren barely audible above the whipping wind. The sky was black. The old barn behind the house had lost its tin roof.

"Good thing the cows and horses are gone, huh?" George said.

He and Mac ran ahead to the storm cellar. The man threw open the door in the large mound of dirt, and the dog shot in. "Hurry up," he yelled. Kate and Emma entered, and he bolted the door shut.

"It's dark, Dad," Emma stated.

"I know, sweetie. I have a flashlight." He pushed a button and shined the light under his face. "Pretty spooky, huh?"

Emma giggled.

"We don't need to waste the batteries though, do we, dear?" Kate scolded.

"I know. I'm pretty sure my grandparents left something down here." George panned the flashlight around the cellar and found a kerosene lantern on a shelf, along with some matches. He lit the lantern, and the cellar filled with soft light.

Kate and Emma sat on two wooden chairs on the other side of the cramped storm shelter, and Mac sat at their feet on the dirt floor. George remained standing. The wind howled outside, rattling the door. Emma clutched her mother's left arm.

"You know," George began, raising his voice above the wind, "when I was about your age, Emma, there was a tornado here when I was visiting my grandparents. We all went in this cellar, and Pappaw told me stories to pass the time."

"What kind of stories?" Emma asked.

"Oh, different things. I can't recall them all right now. One I do remember, though, was about something that happened when Pappaw was young, around Julie's age. He was clearing out some of the trees from the woods around the farm, and he saw a leprechaun."

"Nuh-uh," Emma replied.

"I didn't think so, either, but that's what he said."

"How did he know?"

"He said he saw a little man wearing green wandering around."

Emma furrowed her brow. "Did he get the leprechaun's gold?"

"Nope. He ran after it, but the thing ran off before he could catch it."

The girl laughed. "Do you remember any other stories?"

George walked over to his daughter and crouched in front of her. "He told me the oak tree by the house was magic."

"Was there a leprechaun in it?" Emma wondered.

"No." George said. "I can't remember exactly why, but he told me that as long as that tree stood by the house, everything would be okay. Sure enough, when we got out of the cellar, it was still there. The worst damage was that the wind blew the roof off the chicken coop. Someone a couple of miles down the road found one of the chickens."

"Alive?" Kate asked.

"Well, no. It's hard for something to get sucked up in a tornado and live."

Sudden silence caught the family off guard.

"Can we leave now?" Emma asked.

"Not yet, honey," her mother replied. "We have to wait for the all-clear siren."

They waited quietly for a few moments. Then, an alarm sounded again but died out after about a minute.

"Was that it?"

"Sounded like it," George said. He walked up the steps to the cellar door, unbolted it, and pushed. It didn't budge. He put his shoulder against it and pressed harder. "Huh," he muttered. "It's like something's on the door."

Kate went to her husband. "It might be debris. Here, I'll help." The adults strained against the door, and it popped open. They went outside.

Mac whined.

"What is it, boy?" Emma asked.

Emma's mother turned to her. "Are you coming?"

"Yeah." She bounded up the stairs and stood at the opening. "C'mere, Mac."

The dog put his head down and followed.

The family stood outside the cellar, examining the storm damage. Wind had ripped up the young Bradford pear trees lining the driveway. The old red barn was now demolished. The adults' SUVs were flipped over. Debris littered the yard and busted through the windows of the white farmhouse. The storm had partially uprooted the large tree next to the home, the ancient oak leaning precariously against the roof.

"I'm going to hate telling Julie about this," Kate said softly.

"She doesn't care," Emma snapped. "She doesn't like this place."

Kate sighed. "She does care. The farm is just something new for her. This is still her home, and she'd want to know what happened."

"It won't be so bad," George said cheerfully. "The tree's still up, mostly."

Just then, a branch broke off the tree and scraped against the side of the house.

"Yeah, it could be worse," Kate replied flatly.

They stared at the house. Emma wondered where they would stay and how she could get her things out of her bedroom. Someone could climb a ladder, she thought.

A low moaning cut through the quiet.

"Is it another tornado?" Emma asked. She glanced at the sunny, bright blue sky.

"I don't know," George said. "I thought they gave the all-clear."

"I thought so too," Kate replied.

Mac turned to the direction of the sound and growled.

Emma tried to see what bothered the dog. A pile of debris shifted. A man dragged himself out of the rubble and crawled toward the family. His skin was bluish-gray and covered in cuts and scrapes, and his clothes were tattered. Bones stuck out of the man's broken legs. He reached out and wailed.

"Oh my God, he's hurt," George yelled, running over to the man.

"You don't think the tornado blew him in, do you?" Kate asked.

He didn't answer. Instead, he kneeled in front of the injured man. "Sir, what's your name? Where are you from?" He put his hand out, and the stranger bit off his right ring and little fingers.

George screeched and jumped away. "That son of a bitch bit me."

Emma's face flushed at her father's swearing. She had never heard him say those words before.

He still yelled at the man on the ground. "I was trying to help you!" He kicked the man in the face repeatedly.

"George, stop!" Kate screamed.

He walked back over to his wife and daughter. Blood ran down his arm and dripped onto the ground. "I don't feel well," he said.

"Of course not," his wife replied. "You've lost blood."

Emma looked at her dad. His face was pale, almost white, and there were dark circles under his brown eyes. He was sweating even though it wasn't hot outside. Is he sick? she wondered.

"George looked into his daughter's eyes. "I'm sorry I did that. I was angry. I didn't mean to scare you."

Emma avoided her father's gaze and looked at the man on the ground. He was unfazed by the kicks to the face, continuing to pull himself toward the family. Two figures shuffled behind him. One was a woman in weather-beaten clothes. Her skin was gray, and a piece of brown siding protruded from her left leg. Emma looked back to the white house. Where did the brown come from? the girl wondered. She couldn't tell if the other figure was male or female. It was about her height, though, so she thought it might be a kid. It was rotten, no skin on its face.

Fear stole the voice from her throat. Mac began to bark.

Her parents ignored the dog. "We need to get you some help," Kate said, still examining her husband's hand.

"Mom," Emma croaked. She tugged on her mother's sleeve.

Kate and George looked up and saw the other strangers.

"Hey, what are you doing?" George said weakly. He walked a few steps toward them and fell to the ground.

Kate cried out and reached for her husband.

"I'm okay," he whispered.

The others shambled toward the family, moaning and hissing. A twig snapped behind Emma, and she turned. Two more people headed in their direction.

"What are you doing?" Kate screamed. "What do you want?"

They didn't seem to hear her, continuing to shuffle and reach out to them. The people approached from all sides, standing between the family and the storm cellar.

"What do we do?" Kate asked.

George picked up a tree limb and slowly stood. "Take Emma and run." He spoke, almost in a whisper. "I'll hold them off."

"I can't."

"Kate, go," he said sternly.

He swung at a woman behind Emma and Kate. The tree limb connected with her head, and she fell to the ground. She tried to rise, but George hit her again, harder. He struggled to catch his breath. "Now run," he bellowed.

"Where?" Kate screamed.

"Can't we go in the woods?" Emma asked.

"There might be more of them in there. We'll hide in the house."

Emma didn't like that idea. She knew the tree leaning on the house wasn't safe, and she thought she heard beams cracking under the weight. If her mom believed it was a good idea, though, it must've been one.

"Come on, honey," Kate said, pulling her daughter toward the damaged house. The woman whistled for Mac, and the dog ran toward them.

"Come get me, you bastards," George snarled.

Emma heard the crunch of wood connecting with the flesh and bone. The creatures' groans grew louder. Her father screamed. She turned her head. The monsters kneeled over her father, tearing into his flesh and stuffing chunks into their mouths.

"Don't look back," her mother said.

Too late, Emma thought. "I don't think those things are people," she said.

"Of course they are. What else would they be?"

Emma looked to her left. A body of a woman lay on its back near the driveway. It was gray and windblown like all the others, but it didn't move. A large chunk of a two by four jutted out of its left eye socket.

Kate, Emma, and Mac ran onto the porch. The wind had blown the front door away, and Emma wondered if the back door was gone, too. They entered the house. The lights were out. Glass shards littered the floor, and pieces of shattered furniture were strewn around the house.

"Where do we go, Mom?" Emma whispered.

She didn't respond, looking around the house. Groans emanated from the back. Two of the creatures stood in the kitchen, staring ahead vacantly. When they saw the family, they shambled straight into the dining room. Boxes and old furniture blocked them in.

"Let's hope they're too dumb to use the other door," Kate said.

One of the monsters grunted behind them. Fresh blood dripped from its decayed jaws and ran down the front of its body. Kate pushed Emma ahead of her and ran up the stairs. Mac followed.

Two of the grotesque things awaited them on the second floor.

"How'd they get here?" Kate wondered.

Emma looked past the intruders and peered through the open door of her parents' bedroom. The large window above the bed was shattered. She silently pointed.

"Dear God."

They limped forward while four more shuffled up the stairs.

"What do we do now?" the girl asked.

"You need to hide somewhere, Emma."

26

"I can't leave you, Mommy."

"You have to." Kate grabbed Emma and pushed her into the spare bedroom. Mac followed a few seconds later, and the door slammed shut.

Emma reached for the doorknob, but it wouldn't turn. "What are you doing?"

"I'm keeping you safe, baby girl. Push something against the door."

The girl saw an old wooden chair. She scooted it over and placed it under the doorknob. "I did it," she said.

"Okay," her mom called from other the side, yelling over the moans. "Now, lock the door."

"But you won't be able to get in."

"I know."

"What?"

"I love you, Emma."

"Mommy?"

The moans grew louder, and Kate shrieked. Ripping flesh replaced the creatures' moans. Emma sank to the floor, sobbing. Mac whined and nuzzled her, as if he was trying to comfort her.

After a few minutes, the moans returned. Something bumped against the door. The dog growled. There was another bump, and the chair fell to the floor with a clack.

"They're trying to get in," Emma whispered. She moved toward the door to put the chair back under the doorknob. The things outside kept trying to get in, straining the lock. I have to go, she thought.

Emma meandered through the stacks of boxes and antiques to the other side of the room. The damaged tree outside blocked the window, and the branches smashed in the glass. A yellowed string hung from the attic door in the ceiling. She jumped for it, but it swayed out of her grasp. Boards creaked under her feet. She jumped again and latched onto the string, pulling the door open. The stairs thundered down, and she gasped in surprise. The bedroom door crashed open behind her.

She ran up the steps and peered down. Mac whimpered at her from the floor. "C'mere, Mac," she commanded.

The dog whined again.

"C'mon. We don't have anywhere else to go."

27

He ran up the steps. Just as his front paws reached the attic floor, a gray hand grabbed one of his back legs. Mac yelped and tried to bite his attacker.

No, he'll fall, Emma thought. She wrapped an arm around the front of Mac's body. He struggled against her. "I'm trying to help you," she screamed.

The monster groaned and pulled on the dog.

Emma looked around for a weapon. Something shiny beckoned to her from inside an old, partially opened sewing box. She reached inside and retrieved a pair of black-handled shears that still looked sharp. She stabbed the creature's rotten arm a few times. Soon, the dog was free, although the hand still clung to his back leg. She pried it off and tossed it out the opening.

The girl closed the door and scrambled to the other side of the attic. She wedged herself against a wall, pushing boxes in front of her. Warm, musty air filled her lungs. The creatures still moved around downstairs, but she thought she was safe for the time being.

"I wonder if there are spiders," she said.

Mac cocked his head to the side.

"Yeah, I know what you're thinking. 'Why are you worried about spiders when people are trying to eat you?' Well, for starters, I'm pretty sure they're not people. People don't go around ripping up and eating each other. Plus, you know how I feel about spiders."

Emma sighed, trying to figure out what to do next. She couldn't live in the attic; there wasn't any food or water. She could try to escape out the small attic window, drop down to the roof, and jump to the ground. No, she decided, that won't work. I could hurt myself, and those things are probably still in the yard.

"I think we're stuck, Mac."

The attic floor creaked under her.

"What was that?"

The dog backed away as the floor groaned louder.

Before Emma could move, the boards gave way, and she fell to the second story. She hit the floor hard, knocking the air out of her. Boxes and debris fell after her, and she shielded her head and face. Something human shaped landed on top of her. She yelped and pushed it away. An old dress form hit the floor beside her.

She tried to move her toes, remembering a doctor showing her mom how. The thought of her mother brought tears, but she bit her lip, focusing on the pain instead. As far as she could tell, she wasn't seriously hurt.

Mac jumped from the hole in the ceiling and ran to her. He took her shirt in his mouth and pulled, trying to free her from the rubble. She pushed the beams and plaster off and stood. She had cuts and scrapes on her exposed arms and legs, and her right knee hurt, but she thought she was okay.

She looked around at the familiar, butter yellow walls. How'd I end up in my room? she wondered. Despite the rubble and a couple of shattered windows, it didn't look too bad.

Emma heard gunshots outside and clambered to the window above her desk. Two figures stood beside an old red pickup in the front yard. Mrs. Dean, the neighbor from down the road, was there, her gray hair tied up in a messy bun. Blood stained her apron and the front of her flowered dress. Her fourteen-year-old grandson, Seth, stood next to her. His blond hair, his white t-shirt, and his jeans all carried traces of gore. The Deans aimed their rifles at the creatures that shambled toward them. Bodies littered the yard.

"Help!" Emma shouted.

The old woman pointed her hunting rifle at the girl, who was too stunned to move. Seconds later, a bullet whizzed past her head. Drops of liquid landed on her cheek, and then something thudded behind her. One of the creatures was now on the wooden floor, a smoking bullet hole in its head.

"You okay, Emma?" Mrs. Dean called from the yard.

"Y-Yeah."

"Can you get to your room?"

"Yes, ma'am. That's where I am now."

"Good. I want you to pack up as much stuff as you can carry. I'm sending Seth to come get you."

Emma nodded and ran over the debris to her closet. She pulled out a large suitcase and set it on the floor.

"Why you sendin' me for, Meemaw?" Seth asked outside.

"You're younger and quicker."

"What about the tree?"

"You'll be fine as long as you hurry. Here, take this." There was a momentary pause. "The pistol's better in all that mess. Use the back door. I'll distract them. Now, go. We ain't got all day." A few moments later, the old woman shouted. "Come out here, you stinkin' sacks of pus."

Emma threw clothes inside the suitcase. She noticed her doll exactly where she left it on her bed. Much of the moaning had moved outside, and the girl guessed Mrs. Dean took care of those monsters, but there were also gunshots downstairs. I hope they aren't finding too many. I don't want anyone to get hurt because of me. Doll now in hand, she went back to the suitcase. She tossed the toy inside and zipped the suitcase shut.

Something moved outside her bedroom door. "I'm in here, Seth," she yelled, double-checking her closet for things to take.

Mac growled as the door slowly creaked open.

"What's wrong, boy?" She looked up, expecting Seth. Instead, she saw the bloodied, mangled corpse of her mother. Her right shoulder was dislocated, the arm hanging limply at her side. Large chunks of her neck were gone, and the bottom of her ribcage and her backbone were visible. Kate shuffled toward her daughter.

"Mommy, no," Emma whispered. Hot tears ran down her cheeks.

Mac barked more ferociously.

The girl picked up part of a beam that had once supported the ceiling. She waved it around. "Go away," she sobbed.

Kate stepped closer.

Mac lunged at Kate, but Emma kicked him away. "I can't let you get hurt, too," she yelled.

Her mother was a few feet away, reaching for her.

Emma hit Kate in the head with the beam a few times, but nothing happened. I'm too small and weak to do anything, she thought. She then remembered the dead one (the really dead one) that had a big piece of wood sticking out of its eye socket.

Kate snarled and clutched Emma's left arm.

She pushed the piece of wood through her mother's eye. What had once been Kate stopped moving. Emma used all of her strength to send the body crashing to the floor.

Seth stood in the doorway, wide-eyed. "Jeez, Emma," he blurted.

"Where were you a couple of minutes ago?"

"I was tryin' to get up here." Seth stared at the corpse. "Was that your momma?" he asked quietly.

"Yeah."

"Sorry."

"I-Is she dead?" she whispered.

"Probably. Zombies don't play possum."

Zombie? She knew that word. "It can't be."

"Tell that to them." There was a loud cracking sound outside the room. "We gotta go. It ain't safe here." Seth grabbed Emma's hand while she clutched her suitcase. Mac cut ahead of them as they carefully traversed the ruined house and went outside.

Emma blinked in the sunshine. They walked toward the truck. Mrs. Dean looked at the girl's leg and placed her finger on the gun's trigger.

"You get bit?" she asked calmly.

Emma noticed the blood coming from her knee. "No. I just got cut on a piece of wood or something."

"You sure?"

"Yes, ma'am. Do you know what's going on?"

"The dead walk the Earth."

Emma stared blankly at Mrs. Dean.

"Ain't you ever seen a zombie movie before?" the old woman asked.

"That's all fake, though."

"Apparently not."

"How do you know?"

Mrs. Dean snorted. "The twister dropped them off at my house. They got a hold of one of my cows. Made an awful mess. After we took care of them, Seth saw through this binoculars that y'all's farm was pretty tore up. I thought we should see if y'all were okay."

Emma didn't say anything.

"I'm guessin' not."

She just shook her head.

"What happened?" Seth asked.

"When we got out of the storm cellar, there were a bunch of those...zombies in our yard. They attacked Dad and followed Mom and me into the house."

Mrs. Dean put a hand on Emma's shoulder. "I'm so sorry, honey. Seth and I'll take you to our house till we can figure something out."

The girl's eyes widened. "Is your phone working?" she asked.

"Off and on," Mrs. Dean replied. "Why?"

"I need to call my sister."

"Oh. All right."

"Unless the zombies got her, too." She hung her head.

"Your sister's fine," Seth said, smiling slightly. "Don't worry."

The children and the dog followed Mrs. Dean to the truck.

"You have binoculars?" Emma asked.

Seth blushed and pulled down the tailgate. Mac jumped in. The boy placed the suitcase next to the cab. Emma crawled into the pickup, and the Deans sat on either side of her. Mrs. Dean started the engine.

The vehicle rambled down the bumpy, muddy road toward the Deans' gray farmhouse. Emma looked in the rearview mirror. Mac stood on the wheel well, his tail wagging and his tongue sticking out. She smiled a bit and looked back to her house. A figure shambled in the yard. She couldn't be sure because of the distance, but she thought it wore the remnants of her father's clothes. She gasped.

"What's wrong?" Mrs. Dean asked.

Her eyes went back to the house. The figure wasn't there anymore. "N-Nothing, Mrs. Dean."

Emma looked at the floorboard, tears filling her eyes. She wiped them away before they fell. She had lost her parents and her home, but she still had people who cared about her. She had Mac. Julie was out there somewhere. Most importantly, she was still alive. She would be all right because she survived the storm.

THE COLLECTORS

by Fallon N. Stoeffler

Fallon N. Stoeffler has degrees in fiction writing from the University of Pittsburgh and Education and Psychology from Old Dominion University. She has published a few stories, which can be found at various literary journals online. She lives with her family in Virginia.

I awoke with vertigo so strong it dumped me out of bed. My head was foggy, my ears were ringing. How had I gotten home? The last thing I remembered was that huge, hungry fire, but how had I escaped?

...the robotic chirp of my alarm drew me more into the conscious world. It was 8:25 by my cell phone. My head was a bowling ball on my shoulders. The ringing in my ears started to fade, leaving in its place a rushing sound I associated with mornings after loud concerts and fireworks shows.

I wiped the phone's display and noted that it was Saturday, January 26th. A light flashed as a reminder of some appointment I was late for and I tapped the screen to access it.

"9 a.m.: Meet J @ Aunt L's."

I shook my head, then rubbed each eye in turn with my fists. They burned, like I'd slept with my contacts in.

January 26th had been the day before. I remember because I'd woken up extra early for a Saturday and gone for a run with Grundy, my dog, until he and I were both panting. Then I'd gone to the house to meet my cousin. That was yesterday. January 26th. By all accounts, my phone should have been telling me it was the 27th.

Then the pretty blonde news anchor on my TV was reciting: "We'll be right back with the rest of your news for this Saturday, January 26th," and my mind spiraled backward.

I ran to the bathroom. My knees throbbed with each step. Upon examination I found two large and raw-looking patches of scraped-off skin with chunks of white rock embedded. Tiny drops of blood welled.

My face in the bathroom mirror was puffy and almost shining red, the way a face looks after one's been sitting around a campfire for a few hours.

It had been that enraged, intense fire, which seemed bent on consuming but in which those dead things moved, white-hot phantoms taking final death strolls. I had tried to run but had tripped, landing face down on a sidewalk. That explained my knees. Then the glass had exploded, shards like daggers flying at us in slow motion.

My phone began to sing AC/DC in my hand and I answered.

"January 26th?" The caller said.

"Yeah."

"Did we dream all of that?"

"I don't think so," I responded. "Or else we had the exact same dream."

"Meet you at the house at 10," the voice told me.

I guessed we were going back.

***

January 26th – the first time.

When my eccentric, hoarder aunt died, she left her house and all of its contents to be split by me and Josh, my only cousin. We were instructed to go in and take inventory together and from there, divvy up what we wanted or sell the rest. I'd shown up with a small steno pad and pen, no idea what was in store.

I was seated on a makeshift chair of newspapers from 1993, already overwhelmed. I 'd shown up with one cup of coffee and a small steno pad, but the sight which had greeted me had been so overwhelming I'd remained in one place until my pig-faced cousin stumbled in.

"What a fricking mess," he blurted.

"Good morning, Josh,"

On a list of people I didn't want to spend a day with, Josh was second only to Adolf Hitler.

I took a sip of my coffee and gestured at the stacks of items. "It's obviously quite organized, not really a mess."

Josh puffed air out of his mouth, deflating. "Okay, organized mess. Are you finished here?"

I wasn't sure if he meant with my coffee, or giving him a hard time.

"Yep," I said. "I got here ten minutes ago, organized all of this stuff, and took full inventory including the treasure chests of precious stones and diamonds in the back room. Congratulations, you're a millionaire." I stood, put my hands on the small of my back, and stretched.

He inched closer, staying out of reach like he was afraid I'd throw hot coffee at him. He was standing in a section comprised of three stacked pyramids of different operators' manuals, whereas I was dwarfed by skyscrapers of Readers' Digests, Vogue, old Good Housekeeping, even a modest collection of Playboy in one corner. The periodicals took up nearly half the living room. I stepped out into a walkway made of white taped lines on the floor and moved toward Josh. "At least we're not walking over piles of garbage or finding dead cats underneath piles of baby clothes like in that TV show."

"What's that smell?" He asked. An unmistakable waft of Parliament Menthols usually followed him like a shadow. It was an aggressive odor, striking out on its own when he was around, leaving his side to deliberately chase down and surround anyone in his vicinity.

"You." I wrinkled my nose. Wasn't that the pot calling the kettle smelly?

"No, really." He inched closer, so we were as nose to nose as could be, limited to a five inch gap between us by his burgeoning stomach. I felt moments away from wedgie/noogie territory. "It's something else...kind of chemical smell."

I sniffed at the air, swishing my hand in front of my face to dispense the menthol phantasm and moved on.

"Well, I suggest we do the living room last."

"Fine," Josh agreed, for once, giving the cramped space a visual once-over.

You could see what was in the room by visual alone, and in addition to book stacks were also those of VCR tapes, Laserdisc Player discs, and cartridges for endless video game iterations. A fortress made out of shoe boxes domed the TV, sofa, and loveseat. A variety of lamps created a tiny border line of luminaries along the walls. There was more here than what I remembered in the last of my visits as a girl.

"This is way creepy," Josh said, spokesman for the blatantly obvious.

The house was a ranch with a pretty standard layout; living room, kitchen behind it, long thin hallway with a few doors on either side and one at the end. I started toward the hallway. "Don't worry, princess," I snarked, "It will be over soon."

Through the first door we found a banana-yellow painted guest room filled with hundreds of boxed appliances which were stacked carefully into a huge pyramid.

"Two more," I said, as I jotted down the contents on my notepad, eager to leave the small space which smelled of chemicals and Josh's cigarettes.

The corridor was covered with at least a hundred photo frames, which still displayed the stock photos they were sold with. A young couple with a dog, multiple women in wedding dresses, and a few blonde kids all smiled down at us.

"Replacement family." Josh said. Both his words and their meaning made me shiver. "One for the inventory."

Looking down the hallway reminded me of a funhouse mirror, of looking into an odd-world version of reality. Ahead of us, the hallway looked wider than before. At first, Josh (and I, for that matter) had seemed too large for the small passage. It might have been my imagination, but we now fit side-by-side.

"We should just quit," he blurted.

I gave him a look.

"Fine." He threw his hands up in surrender and stepped closer. "Let's get it over with, then."

There was another perceptual trick happening: the hallway was not only wider, but longer. A few minutes ago, it had spanned maybe ten feet from start to finish. Now we were halfway down, and it was at least five feet just to the next door, and what looked like another fifteen or twenty from there to the end.

"Huh."

"What?" Josh asked, his question a tight cluster of hard consonants as he looked at me again with a face asking for reassurance of normalcy.

I didn't have any to give him except to ignore what he thought he was seeing, and I just shook my head. "Next room."

The smell hadn't abated at all in here. Now it had top notes of a strong plastic smell, thick and rubbery. Late morning sun came through a window covered with bent and broken blinds to light the room's contents, which consisted of deep Tupperware containers, stacked three high in places and covering the floor. Inside of them were hundreds of dolls, separated by body parts.

Mutilated body parts.

The right and left arms were all missing thumbs.

Left legs were missing all of their toes but the big toe.

Right legs were missing only pinkie toes.

The torsos were [vivisected].

The heads were all missing the eyes.

I felt trapped in a little girl nightmare, one where my playthings had come to life to attack me. I waited for the dolls to draw their horribly mangled bodies together and chase us.

"So what do I write down for this?"

With no answer to my hanging question, we backed out of the door on tender feet, as if silence would keep the dolls in their boxes, asleep.

"Is it me," Josh took in our surroundings, "Or did the hall just get..."

"Longer? Wider?" There was even more room now; we were standing abreast of each other with space between us and still not touching the sides. Down the corridor, there was now at least thirty feet to the last door, and two more had appeared, one on each side.

"It's not just you," I answered. If we both saw it, then clearly our imagination had not changed these dimensions, but something else did, something outside of us. Around us, the light dimmed, though sunset was still more than seven hours away.

There was also another thing I wasn't saying aloud. Josh, who had been both taller and wider than me since we were teens, was looking up at me with a face that was younger, softer, and childishly trusting and vulnerable.

"We...we should keep going?"

I nodded my affirmation and noticed that we were now both drowning in our clothes. Our adult garments were too loose for what had become suddenly child-sized bodies.

What the hell was happening here?

Josh indicated the door to the left. "This one first? I think it may be a bathroom."

It was a bathroom, an outdated one. Shiny, art-deco style black and white tiles covered the floor and climbed most of the way up the walls, and it gave the dizzying illusion of walking into a magic eye puzzle. A cracked claw-footed tub was concealed by a shower curtain in one corner; a matching sink stood alone on an opposing wall with a bronze-framed mirror over it.

"Look at this," I breathed. Across the mirror, from top to bottom, was written over and over:

ALLMINE

The tiny letters cramped into every single space of the warped and reflective glass. When I stood right in front of it, I noticed that between it and a wall-length mirror behind me, I appeared trapped in an entire room full of those terrible red words.

ALLMINEALLMINEALLMINEALLMINE.

Josh wasn't looking. He was reaching instead for the shower curtain. A thousand horror-movie and novel scenes clattered in my mind, and I was expecting to see a dead, rotted thing behind there. My vision tunneled in on the bathtub, the fear so palpable that the air felt hard to breathe. I wanted to tell Josh to stop, didn't he know that was always a bad idea. I fought an urge to scream and a stronger one to flee, but as in a nightmare, my mouth was dry, my legs and vocal chords locked.

Metal on metal scraped as he drew the curtain back.

I found my voice, cried out while Josh retched loudly and without abandon, creating a cacophony. My rational self screamed at me. You're not here! It's your imagination! You're still sitting on those front stacks of newspapers! You're still outside the front door! You're still in bed and dreaming!

The tub was filled with fingernails. It looked like someone had bought out the stock of Press-On nails at every Wal-Mart in America, in every color, and dumped them into the tub.

Except Press-On nails didn't come with jagged pieces of skin attached. These did.

Josh was still throwing up, and I didn't fault him. No one knows how they are going to react to a surplus of fingernails until they see thousands of them at once in a bathtub.

I could imagine that there were hundreds of hands in that bathtub, hands shooting up from deep, black water to be saved from drowning.

They started to move, crackling and clicking as they tapped against each other. It could have been the house moving, but I was sure it was just them. That any moment they'd scatter and click away, searching out their host fingers.

"Oh my dear God, I have to get out of here!"

Josh, swiping at his mouth with his shirt, followed as I backed out of the door. He looked so young now, a boy's body with a man's brain in his head. In whatever this house was or had become since we'd last been here, I thought our fear might make us more and more child-like until we were irreversible. Josh's bowling-ball head connecting with my gut knocked us both into the hall and out of the bathroom. The smell was again intense and pervasive, acrid. My nostrils and throat were beginning to sting.

"What is all of this?" Josh choked out, trying to breathe and talk. "I get...newspapers and maybe the boxes...but boxes of mutilated dolls...bathtub... fingernails?" His machine-gun prattle echoed my own frightened and confused thoughts.

Were we even in the right house? It was a nonsensical thought, a child's attempt at reassigning blame. "This can't be Aunt Loretta's house. She was always so...so... nice." I said aloud, coughing, a coppery blood-taste in my throat.

"Was she?" Josh patted me on the back as he labored to regain his own breath. "We haven't been here in years. We barely knew her except a few college visits after...." He broke off that thought and began again. "Why did we have to dig through this stuff? Why did she want us to see this?"

There wasn't anyone else, I wanted to say. That was why. Because when Josh and I were 16 and 18, respectively, everyone else had died.

My parents had waited until well into their thirties to reproduce and by that time only had time for one child. Mom's sister, Loretta, had been one of two surviving siblings, and my Dad had just one brother. He and his wife had produced only Josh. This had made up our whole extended family.

A severe case of empty-nester syndrome had driven my parents to plan a big family trip when I'd been midway through my first semester, when I was feeling the weight of impending biology midterms, chemistry experiments gone awry, and a threatened GPA. Big, bulky Josh hadn't been able to take a week out of football, picked for the varsity as a junior at a school which was frequented by college recruiters. He'd dreamed of playing for Ohio State, then someday professionally, so our family, minus us, had headed for sunny Mexico.

"...only one came back," I whispered.

I thought of my eccentric Aunt Loretta. I had known her as a kid, before Mom had demanded we stopped coming. After the trip, my aunt Loretta had visited from time to time, always with a gift and the promise that she would take care of us.

"What?" Josh's question pulled me out of my reverie.

"I was just thinking about the trip," I said. "I was thinking how strange it was that you and I couldn't go, everyone else in the entire family went, and only Aunt Loretta came back."

41

"Aunt Loretta." His voice was shriller than it should have been for a man closing in on 30. He stared past and through me, scanning his memories. "She started to visit me after. Brought me stuff, told me she'd take care of me..." he faltered, choked up. "Do you think...I mean..."

"I don't know," I answered. The deaths had been ruled accidental; their snorkeling boat had overturned, and they were pinned underwater by the bench seatbelt they'd been wearing. I understood what he was now implicating. "No way. That's crazy. "

"Stranger things have happened," Josh said. "When did you ever think you'd find a room full of vivisected and mutilated doll parts?"

Good point.

We were nearly eye-level again and I thought as well as saw it in his eyes – no way did we want to walk into any more rooms. We'd already tried and convicted Aunt Loretta in both of our minds of an unspeakable crime, but neither of us wanted to say it out loud or give credence to it. I couldn't fathom that this woman had been not only eccentric, but crazy enough to kill six family members on a boating trip.

If they'd died on a boating trip.

"Last room?" I asked.

"Last room," Josh said, and surprisingly, took my hand in his. Our palms were clammy.

Overcome by vertigo, I squeezed my eyes shut, watched tiny fireworks explode behind the lids, and reopened them. The hallway appeared to settle and together, we advanced on the next door, grasped the handle, and pushed it open.

I saw what I first mistook as faceless mannequins before realizing what they really were.

This was where it all turned; where I'd been lost.

Under a dim and flickering overhead light was a room full of white, faceless orbs, which seemed to float in midair but were actually poised on black metal rods attached to the floor. They were head forms, like the kind used to hold wigs, and over each was a hairpiece. Men's, women's, permed, straight, even plaited auburn pigtails. As I approached one of the wigs, that chemical smell became so strong I nearly doubled over. Examining, I saw that from under the hair, a brown women's bob, protruded bits of a translucent, sheet like substance, like raggedly torn paper.

Like skin.

Like a scalp.

A tiny rivulet of blood had run down the head form from under the hair and dried some amount of time ago.

Who knew how long they'd all been here?

"Oh my god," I moaned. "Josh, these are real. Real... scalps." I'd long since dropped his hand and now moved freely from one to the other. "Oh my god, oh my god," I whispered this over and over to myself as a protection mantra.

In my fear, the twenty or so faceless heads seemed to stare and whisper at me: Get out. Get out of our place. This is where we keep our watch. This is where we hold court.

"D-d-did she d-do this to them?" Josh asked. The stutter he'd had as a kid, which there'd been no trace of since, was resurfacing.

Was it plausible? I had to wonder where she'd gotten all of this stuff from. The room full of appliances. The items in the rest of the house were not stuff anymore but parts of people; fingernails, scalps.

I moved toward three mannequin heads to my left, those nearest the door. One was nondescript men's hair... a blonde-brown color, longish, with a cowlick in back. The other was thin and gray, so thin I could see the mutilated scalp underneath in large patches. The last one was a neat, black bob. Familiar hair, hair I'd helped to brush and twirled around my fingers. It was a beautiful raven-black, a color I remembered other people coveting.

I reached out, not being able to help myself, and touched it. I felt my sanity crack a little, right down the middle. "Jesus. Oh, dear God. Mom." I moaned over and over again.

The room began to physically spin then in its foundation, like a carnival tilt-a-whirl. Things outside the window whizzed past. Josh grabbed my hand right before my sanity dissolved completely, and I lost consciousness.

"We should g-get out of huh-huh-here!" It was suddenly hard to hear him over the din around us, which was like a buzzing sound, like a swarm of ten thousand killer bees.

"What is this?" I screamed at him.

"I don't know! Let's get out of here!"

One of the mannequin head stands fell over and we scrambled for each other.

We ran into the hallway, which now appeared to have taken on a thirty degree length. I wanted to leave, needed to leave. I had an idea that if I stayed too long in this house, I would start to think crazy, murderous thoughts.

I'd already wondered what Josh's thick, brown hair would look like on one of those...

I shook my head, clearing it. I was heading in the direction of the living room and toward freedom when Josh yanked me back.

"I have to see the last room."

Terror and exasperation filled my words. "Why?"

"I have to!" He yelled. "I have to know if there's anything else!" He started to run, but it was like watching someone in a dream; his upper body seemed far ahead of his feet, which were moving as if wading through mud.

I followed, feeling as if I too were wading through tar. So strong was the chemical smell back here that I felt like I was breathing needles into my lungs. I thought of those scalps and how well-preserved they'd been.

Just like that, it clicked.

"Formaldehyde!" I yelled up to Josh. "That's the smell!"

He stopped and turned.

"That's why everything is in such good shape! That smell! It's formaldehyde!" I remembered from college biology that formaldehyde was used to preserve bodies, because it had firming effects on body tissue. Maybe Aunt Loretta hadn't been some crazy witch, just an extremely thorough caretaker.

Something my mom had said once occurred to me.

"We're not going to go to Aunt Loretta's anymore." She'd been fixing peanut butter sandwiches.

"Why, Mommy? I like Aunt Loretta."

"Me too, sweetie. I just don't think it's a good place for...you. Too dangerous."

I stood up on shaky, bleeding legs, wincing at the flex of my joints where the skin broke open further. I wanted more than anything to close my eyes, to wake up from a horrible nightmare, but it's never a nightmare when you want it to be.

"Josh," I croaked at him, trying to draw breath through what felt like a millimeter wide hole in my throat. "Josh, where's your lighter?" I kept one eye trained on the house the entire time as I said this; saw the faceless faces coming into the windows, walking blindly around the horrific house, toppling over piles of stuff.

He looked at me, and realization dawned. "All of that stuff....it's..."

"It's flammable!" I scratched out. "And all of that paper in there...held together with glue! Glue and formaldehyde! Throw it in there!"

Josh scrabbled for his pants pocket, a cargo pocket near his knees on his pants. He dug around and pulled out a thin, long stick, which didn't look like a lighter. Then he flipped a switch and saw that it was not only not a lighter, but a cigar torch...one that stayed on and produced a high flame with a white-hot center.

"Throw it!"

He steadied up in front of the door, positioning himself in front of it like a pitcher on a pitcher's mound, wound up, and delivered a baseball-perfect pitch which sent the torch end over end, directly between the two figures coming near the door. It landed in front of the periodicals I'd sat on when I first came in, and then the pile caught fire with a low "whoosh" sound.

I didn't know if the house would slow burn, or go up suddenly, but I didn't want to be around when either happened. "That was great!" I breathed, and pulled him away from the house. We ran to his car, got inside of it. I could get a new car, I didn't care. We were both going to leave here together.

Josh backed out of the driveway as I watched flames lick the ceiling of the living room through the open door, saw the arm of the first figure first smolder and then light up brightly as the chemical-soaked limbs caught.

"Sorry, Mom," I whispered, and a tear slipped down my face.

Maybe it was my imagination, but I thought I saw a head nodding within that fire.

This is when it all exploded.

***

September 26th. (Again.)

I relived it as I drove, with more fear than ever that the house would still be there and I'd be endlessly looped into a purgatory involving the nightmare place.

I found nothing, however, but the rubble of a burned-up building. The cinder block slab foundation was blackened, the frame only ash. A smoky haze had replaced it, its terrible smell one which could be created only when furniture, paper, chemicals, and people burned in symphony.

A truck rumbled behind me, and by the time I'd turned, Josh was bounding from it and running toward me. For the first time in probably twenty years, we hugged.

"Oh dear god," he gushed, "I thought I was crazy. I thought I dreamed everything."

His face and upper arms were as angry and red as mine. Pinprick spots on his face and the backs of his hands advertised a run-in with some shattered glass.

He saw my eyes assess him and gestured back toward the truck. "The windshield imploded," he said.

When I didn't say anything, he launched. "Do you know what this even was? What this even was about? Because for the past four hours, I've been thinking only about this and what happened...what we saw here. Was it real?"

I nodded. "It was real, but I think only to you and me. We both have the bruises to prove it." I looked at the rubble, at the truck with its missing windshield, and at my own knees, mummy-wrapped in thick gauze. "But...I don't think anyone else would ever believe it was real."

"I know it was," Josh was defensive. "I saw ...those people. I know they were here."

I took his hand and sandwiched it between my own. "It was, Josh. I can't...." I started to say I couldn't explain it, because I couldn't. Because while we'd both seen those creatures, only I had seen the one who had once been my mother, and had heard them talking in my head. I never finished the explanation.

My eye caught sight of something gleaming in the middle of the rubble and I halted mid-sentence to go investigate. In the area which had probably been one of those nightmare rooms in that fun-house hallway, I cleared a board and a handful of soot and uncovered a small box.

Josh was behind me. "What is it?"

I reached out and touched it, not sure of what it was made of (it appeared to be metal), sure it would singe my finger, but it didn't. It was only slightly warm. The lid wasn't locked, only connected on one of four sides by hinges. I pulled it back, and breathed in.

"Needles and thread," I said quietly.

"What?" He nearly screeched.

I turned and held the box out. "It's sewing stuff," I said, showing him the bloody inside of the box. Inside were three long, thick, and dangerously pointy needles and sturdy thread. Like something you would use to sew a tarp together.

Or piece human bodies back together.

Josh turned and walked away. "Fuck that," he said over his shoulder. "Fuck on all of that."

I followed him with the box in tow. I didn't know how to explain what had happened at the house, but now, seeing it burnt down, gone, I felt a little better.

"It's yours now," the voice in my head said, stopping me in my tracks. I felt warm, removed from myself, hypnotized.

I'm listening. The voice in my own head responded, surprising me.

"It's all yours."

I found myself smiling and thinking about the needle and thread. How useful it might be. The box hummed a little, vibrated in my arms and made me feel energized in a way I'd never felt before.

How nice to have something passed down through the family.

I set the box on the seat beside me, opened it, and stuck one of my hands in. I caressed the needle and it bit back, pricking my fingertip painfully. I lifted it to my lips, tasted blood there. I felt myself zoning out again, the sound dropping away, seeing my mother as that dead, posed mannequin among the rubble.

"You don't have to be alone," a voice said.

Had I misunderstood Aunt Loretta? Had she just need some companionship?

Before I knew what I was doing, I stood up and heard myself shout.

"Hey Josh!"

"Yeah?" He stuck his head out of the driver's side window, straining over the sounds of the idling diesel.

"Why don't you come over for dinner tonight," I said. "We'll have a few drinks and talk about it."

He shook his head, rolled his eyes. "Deal," he shouted back at last.

I got in the car, smirking, stuck my hand back in the box. The world was a little blurry around the edges, but that was okay.

At the touch of my hands, the box began to pulse, throb, and buzz. I let them talk to me; all of them.

They were mine now.

TROUBLE WITH THE TOOTH FAIRY

by Victoria Rowe

Victoria Rowe is a freelance artist and writer
currently pursuing a degree in Media Arts and
Animation. Her most recent story is a psychological
flash fiction of a boy with an alter ego in *Mirror,
Mirror* published in *Danse Macabre Online Literary
Magazine*. She currently lives with her family and
two dogs in Frederick, MD while attending school.

Something was missing.

The horror spread through his body at the absence in
his mouth. His fingers crawled to his lips in a hesitant
effort to feel what his tongue could not. A distinct metallic
taste permeated his senses as his fingers broke through
the barriers of his lips. The slippery feel of his gums made
his stomach churn as his fingertips swept over the serrated
tissue where his teeth had been.

It was a mess.

Lucas reeled away from his pillows as the revulsion
spread like a disease, sickening him with dread as to what
had happened. His breath struggled to free itself from his
lungs as tears drowned his eyes, saturating his face as
they spilled over. He choked on the noises he made,
turning every scream into an agonizing sob that caused
more trouble than the effort was worth.

The panic deafened Lucas to the subtle creaking that
shadowed his distress. It started as a groan no louder than
a dull whisper and gradually escalated into a perceivable
threat to Lucas, who found the noise foreign and alarming.

Lucas's cries became reduced to gentle whimpers,
sputtering from his bloody lips as his eyes scanned the
room for the source of the noise. He had become aware too
late and the creaking ceased...momentarily.

The seconds strained like hours before Lucas heard the noise again, growing louder and more confident than previously. He felt like a toy in a game of cat and mouse, before he finally located the source. His closet door announced itself through the noise as it gingerly crept open to reveal the darkness it bore. Lucas felt himself unable to move in its presence and suffered silently even as the creaking stopped and the door halted its leisurely pace. He held his breath as he waited for something, anything, to happen and prayed the anticipation would kill him before whatever opened the door could.

But there was nothing...

Absolutely nothing, except-

Wait.

What the hell was that?

Soft traces of what appeared to be a stark-white face stared back at him through empty eye-sockets. An ambiguous mouth gave no expression as it watched the boy on the bed.

There was a surreal moment beyond the blinking and the mouth faltering that Lucas's breath became ensnared in his throat as he felt the eyes on him. Heavy and daunting.

A sharp inhale provided entry for the blood to slither down his throat and catch the air in his lungs. Sporadic coughs burst through his chest, abruptly waking him from his dark thoughts.

The figure never blinked.

*　　*　　*

Lucas's eyes fluttered open as the light pooled in through the window, revealing the scrawny teenager with his fingers caught in his mouth. Saliva dribbled down his chin as he awkwardly removed all ten digits and wiped them on the blankets he was buried in. He didn't notice the blood staining his fingertips or the cuts that marked where his braces had punctured the flesh. Instead, he remained comforted in his bed's hold as his eyes drifted warily around the room. His soft breathing soothed his pounding heart, and he found the adrenaline beginning to fade with the realization of morning.

Though the composure was fleeting as his alarm clock suddenly burst into its morning ritual, shattering the silence that had brought Lucas some comfort. Irritated and embarrassed at his reaction towards the device, he absently swiped in its direction until he landed the hit and the screeching hushed. Whether for five more minutes or until tomorrow, it brought Lucas back to reality with a sigh. This meant only one thing.

School.

Despite having endured the horror his night brought him, school would progress mundanely as he endured his classes and the vague attempts to pass by those that offered nothing but torment to him.

But what could he do?

He braced himself against their hatred and fled from their grasp whenever an opportune moment presented itself. That day proved no different, and Lucas's saving grace came in the form of a final lunch bell as he retreated to the bathroom. The mirrored walls exposed Lucas's imperfection in his mouth.

He bared his teeth at his reflection and prodded at the metal brackets with a disapproving fingertip. The brackets didn't budge as he knew they wouldn't, and despite his abhorrence for them, he couldn't ignore the small morsel of relief for their enduring presence.

Lucas pulled himself away from his reflection as he took notice of a small package on the ground near one of the bathroom stalls. He approached it cautiously with a subtle glance around to make sure no one else could view his curiosity.

"What the hell?" he muttered. He ran the clear bag through his fingertips, until the plastic tightened around the small bundle of sticks that cluttered the bag. Incense. A few simple sticks of incense bound together in the center by what appeared to be white paper. Curiously, his hands dove through the plastic and caressed the soft feel of the sticks. His fingers briefly hesitated on the paper, before retrieving it and discovering small writing along the inside.

Take from the tooth fairy what you will

but be warned the cost of equivalent exchange.
Caution.
Do NOT burn more than one.
If you're hurt in your dreams, you will actually be
hurt...don't die.

Remember to wake up. His heart pressed against his ribcage, hungry for the words of intrigue the note brought. Lucas removed his bag from his shoulder and securely fit the incense inside while his note took to the shelter of his jeans' pocket. Another bell sounded through the school, and Lucas scurried from the bathroom, unable to conceal the small smile that revealed his braces.

Lucas never noticed the company he had in the bathroom, watching him through two slits in a mask. Its shape was elongated and adorned in black garments, which had molded with age, as it stood to its full height inside the cramped stall. Carefully, it meandered beyond the protection of the feeble walls and approached the mirror, lowering itself to see a reflection. The figure's facial features were obscured by a theater mask, lacking any expression beyond the hints of a smile pressed over taut lips. However, the smile itself was hard to see. The entire mouth was muddled in a red frenzy that censored any details.

By the time Lucas arrived home, the excitement had dwindled, and beyond setting up his new toy, his attention found itself behind a computer screen with large headphones. Music and shouting blared into his ears as he lost himself in a virtual world.

"I gotta bail, man." Lucas sighed at his friend's submission and balanced his cheek on his hand.

"Dude, we've literally got three more missions before we can be upgraded," Lucas muttered.

"Sorry, but I gotta get some sleep. I've got school tomorrow. You should get some sleep too. You've been on way longer than me. Don't you have school too?" Lucas muttered his admittance but merely switched off his headphones as a friend he'd never met logged off. He glanced at the clock in the corner of his screen.

Midnight.

Hours had flown by beyond his control, and he was still wide-awake. The voices through his headphones had diminished periodically through the night and were almost silent until none remained. He leaned back in his desk chair after removing his headphones and brushed his hands through his dark hair, resting them at the top of his head to view his screen. His character waited for him to move, but Lucas had lost the momentum for the game. Sullenly, he logged off his game as his fingers dipped into his pockets, feeling the flimsy texture of the note and revitalizing his enthusiasm. He glanced towards the incense sitting on his dresser and his thoughts became consumed by the possibilities his night held. With night came lack of reason to put it off any further. He needed sleep anyway.

Once dressed for bed he lit the incense and left the note on the table beside his bed, as he crawled beneath the covers. It took a few minutes of adjusting to become comfortable on his bed, but even as he lay there, something just wasn't quite right. It took him a moment to realize his discomfort came from a subtle but pungent odor that began to permeate through his room. It was almost sickening and parched his mouth, leaving a strong desire for water, spit, or anything to give him relief. He looked towards the incense and watched the smoke rising through the air, increasing his discomfort, and accompanied by that smell. That horrendous smell. It was familiar, but out of reach.

Mold...

Garbage...

Rotting...something...

The answer was repulsive in his mouth, and as the sensation of cold fingers gently traced down his spine, he buried himself further into his blankets. It was disgusting scent and he would have put it out too, had he not been just

so...

damn...

tired...

* * *

The dark room felt alive as Lucas's eyes flickered open. He felt his heart racing, but found the cause lacking. Slowly, he pulled himself from the grasp of his pillows as his eyes began to adjust to the darkness of the room. The shadows created the form of familiar shapes as he recognized the setting as his own bedroom. A breath of relief slipped from his lips, but caught short in his lungs as a creaking began to take hold in the bedroom. He told himself that the house had grown weary with age and moaned beneath its own weight, though the lie hardly convinced him as he wrapped the blankets tighter around himself. Lucas remained still until the creaking hesitated and he had his opportunity to feel for the lamp beside his bed. His arm groped the darkness blindly but touched only the cool sensation of the wooden nightstand beyond his fingertips. As he turned to look, the creak returned, growing louder in the silence. Lucas felt petrified as his eyes danced across the shadows for any possible signs of movement as the creaking diminished. Nothing, nothing...

Wait.

Was his closet door open before? No, he checked it before he went to bed. That he was sure of. Lucas slowly felt responsiveness return to his body in the confidence that emerged with the silence. He had to shut the door. That urgency pressed him forward to crawl to the edge of his bed, and caused his heart to stop when the door slowly began to move. It inched slowly, accompanied by the creaking, until nothing but darkness showed in the closet. There was no movement beyond the opening of the door, from Lucas or whatever else occupied the room. Only silence remained. Lucas took a breath as his courage began to return. A thought kept recurring in his mind that if he shut the door, there would be nothing for him to worry about. He played that thought like a track on loop in his mind as he slowly climbed off the bed. His socks graced the wooden floor and let out a moan as his weight lowered. It caught him off guard briefly, but he managed to keep his wits as he slowly dragged his feet along the floorboards, refusing to lift his feet and cause any further noises. As he neared the closet he heard a soft scampering across the floor from a small object, directly behind him. As he glanced around, another pattering noise followed him. Then another, and another. They began to circle him, coming from all around. Lucas inched away, trembling as he did, and unaware that he was being backed further and further into the closet. The dark, dark closet. A shrill crack in the floor brought about silence in the room as Lucas froze and whatever circled him froze as well. With a sharp glance back he realized how close the darkness crept up on him and he jerked away, sprawling himself over the floor. He shut his eyes as he impacted against the wooden boards and as he opened them, something was staring back.

Something very, very small.

Its eyes were dark, black, and beady as they stared at Lucas. Large ears were unfolded from the sides of its head, and a little nose twitched up and down. Lucas could hear its breath and feel the presence of others around him. More began to appear as Lucas maintained and slowly pulled himself to his knees. They gathered around him, whatever they were and stared up at him with their beady eyes.

Watching.

Waiting.

"What the hell are you..." Lucas whispered, beneath his breath. Their ears flickered at the sight of the metal in his mouth, and a few crawled forward on their little paws for a closer inspection. Lucas didn't understand the attraction and gingerly held a finger out to them. One of the creatures hesitantly approached him with a nose extended to his finger. He could feel the small whiskers dancing across his skin as the cold noses breathed in his scent. He pulled his arm back as the comfort began to return and watched as one of the creatures cautiously approached him with a small candy gripped firmly between two miniscule paws. It placed the candy on Lucas's lap and looked up at him expectantly. Lucas brought the candy to his face for closer inspection but found his vision in the darkness was lacking.

"I'm sorry I can't see, I-." His words were caught in his throat as another gremlin emerged, pushing a small flashlight before itself. Lucas gripped the flashlight with his freehand and thumbed around for the button before discovering it on the end of the flashlight. The light illuminated the darkness and gave a more accurate view of the creatures before him. Their bodies were sheltered in a thin layer of fur with the skin still visible beneath the follicles, with ears that outsized their bodies considerably in proportion. Though what drew Lucas's eye were the claws. They were black, sharp and lengthy as they seemingly bore into the floorboards.

"You guys look like gremlins," Lucas whispered breathlessly. One of the creatures gently pawed at his leg with its nose gesturing towards the sweet. Lucas glanced at the wrapper and stifled his alarm. After all, it was just candy. He dug into the wrapper, retrieving the sweet and placed it on his tongue. It was sticky, and remnants of the candy clung to the wiring in his mouth that forced his jaw to extend further as he chewed.

The gremlins never took their eyes off of him; ears fanned out from the side of their heads and eyes widened at the beautiful glimmer of light through his lips.

Take, take, and take. The requests were simple even as they piled one after another, but his intention was far more than candy, light, or any other simple whim. It was the feeling of control. It was beyond satisfying and a feeling Lucas had been starved for so much that he found it intoxicating. These gremlins were incredible creatures, and as Lucas returned to bed with the gremlins tucked safely away in the remnants of his dream, he couldn't help but think what a lucky find.

*   *   *

Lucas sat in his bed with a weight sinking on his chest that proved to be nothing more than disappointment at being alone in his room. His thoughts hung lower than his head as he slid out from the covers with a mournful glance to the tightly shut closet door. His eyes danced around the room briefly, adjusting to the light, before wavering over the incense. It must have gone out at some point last night, but boy did it ever work. He could still feel the gentle tingle of tiny paws crawling all over him and the sensation of those cold noses leaving damp traces of themselves behind. He could still feel the texture of the candy, gritted in between his teeth and metal brackets.

School provided no means of comfort, as Lucas meandered through the halls in a haggard state, feeling the exhaustion weighing on him like a burden. He couldn't even remember how he had gotten there, only that he was there. However, what truly made him uneasy were the students passing him in the hallways. There was something off about them. Something about their disfigured faces, blood-soaked shirts, and deadened eyes.

It was that something that slipped beyond Lucas's perception but remained in his paranoia. Extended glances at the students could dispel the fear-induced images, but Lucas found it too unsettling to attempt. It was better to keep his pace and head lowered.

It's there.

He fleetingly noticed the dark figure as it snaked its way through the crowd. Its attention was focused on the boy through the eyeholes of its mask.

It's nothing.

Lucas ambled through his classes, finding little to focus on and much to ignore, given the appearances of those surrounding him. By the time the lunch bell rang, Lucas mistook it for his alarm clock and swiped at the air around him, causing a few stares from his peers. Realizing what he had done, he awkwardly fled to his locker.

It's closer.

It stood across the hallway from him, cloaked in the shadows, an empty classroom possessed. Always staring. Always through the eyeholes of a mask.

Lucas retrieved his lunch bag and ambled to the cafeteria, attempting to pull himself back to reality without much success. His hunched position and lack of interest made him an easy target.

The mirror revealed a budding black eye that appeared as Lucas stared at his reflection. He had never felt this reaction towards his tormentors and his hate was perplexing. The look in the mirror wasn't simply to study the damage, but as a means to fuel his rage until he got home. When he could be the boss. The gremlins wouldn't fight back. All they did was give.

It's right there.

But Lucas didn't notice that peeping through the stall was the mask, gently fingering the indented smile that had been carved in.

At home, Lucas found his games to be less of a distraction than he had hoped for. The light was still evident outside, and his usual bedtime of midnight was still hours away. A conclusion in his game and a glance in the mirror brought his thoughts back to the gremlins. Maybe he didn't have to wait until midnight. He could go to bed early. An idea struck him, and in his enthusiasm, the note became forgotten. Beside the holder containing the single stick, burned the previous night, was the bag. Lucas carefully removed the remaining few and set them ablaze. He watched the fire take ahold of the tips and let it burn briefly before blowing it away. The smoke rose as did traces of the stench. Lucas fanned the smoke away from himself and crawled into bed to burrow himself under the covers. Unlike the previous night, the stench simply didn't seem as strong. Maybe he was used to it? Though that was an odd thought, since he had only used it once before. He decided to contemplate it later. Right then he was just

so...

damn...

tired...

*   *   *

The anger was residual in Lucas's clenched fists even more so than when he had fallen asleep. However he woke to the pleasant sight of the small gremlins clamoring around his bed, patient for his movement. He pulled himself up without so much a glance to the creatures as they scattered to allow him space. A shaky breath filled his lungs as he attempted to exhale contentment at his return to his little friends.

"Hey guys," Lucas greeted softly. A few of the gremlins crawled to him cautiously, before unfolding their ears in a gesture of comfort to Lucas's presence. Lucas held out a finger and smiled as a few approached him with curious noses.

"You probably smell those bastards on there," he muttered, taking notice of another cut he must've sustained through the encounter. Two of the gremlins placed their tiny paws on Lucas's finger and gently bathed his wound in their saliva. Their tongues tickled and Lucas pulled away, shaking his head. They licked their chops.

"Easy guys. That tickles," he said. They stared up at him, resting on their large hind legs as though they found something curious about how he tasted. Lucas ignored the attention and pet a few of them momentarily before he felt himself past greetings. He had spent all last night with them. Surely they were beyond any formalities.

"Alright guys. Go grab me some cereal, I'm starved," Lucas ordered. The gremlins held their gaze and watched his movements with their beady eyes. Lucas let out a groan and made shooing motions with his hand, but found it was to no avail. The gremlins were firmly seated and held no intention of moving.

"What are you guys? Stupid? Your ears are big enough, I know you can hear me! Come on, I've had a hell of a crappy day," he complained, making an emphatic gesture of throwing his arms in the air with obvious exasperation at their lack of compliance. Finally, two gremlins seated at the foot of his bed leisurely raised themselves to their feet and hopped off the bed to disappear down the dark hall. Lucas watched them leave, muttering a 'finally...' under his breath, as he leaned back against his pillows.

Their return wasn't as prompt as he was expecting, and as they returned, he sneered.

"About time..." he muttered, when the gremlins placed a crumpled bag of goods before him. He dug greedily through the sack and retrieved a small candy identical to the night before.

"This is candy, *not* cereal," he complained, tossing the candy aside. A gremlin crawled up his leg and stared at his mouth, ears twitching. Lucas brushed it off as he reached for the lamp beside him. It flickered. Light spread through the room before quickly being diminished. Damn bulb must be going out.

He didn't notice the illumination on the mask behind the door or the red stain on the chin curved in a smile.

He did notice the paper. The words of warning had been scrawled over in a messy font stating the second line of the note.

Be warned the cost of equivalent exchange

Lucas briefly fumbled with the light before it glinted, casting shadows of the gremlins around him in demonic poses around the room. He brought the note to his face for a closer inspection but tossed it aside. He then crawled out from his covers with a few gremlins hopping on the floor around him. The note lay in a heaped pile on the floor, at the foot of a shadow in the corner of the room. Behind the door.

The sight of the figure brought out a terrible scream from Lucas, who stumbled over a gremlin and in a desperate attempt to grab at something to keep from falling, turned himself over and ended up on his face. He felt the pain throbbing in his mouth and the metallic taste of blood moistening his tongue. He gave no thought to the throbbing and whirled around to face a simple shadow behind his door. No mask, no figure. He sighed and laid his head back on the floorboards. He could feel the gremlins crowding around him and the tickle of the whiskers on his cheeks. He brushed some of them away, but found one had climbed atop his chest and peered down at him, resting on his chin.

"Mo-." Lucas never finished the word. The last word he'd ever speak and he didn't even get to finish it. The gremlin let out a deafening screech with its ears pressed flat against its body. Its lower jaw unhinged, extending further to reveal rows and rows of tiny, sharp teeth, bathed in saliva. Lucas had no time to react as it bit into his lower lip and tore it clean off to expose the teeth. Several other gremlins leapt on him, and sunk their jagged teeth into his flesh. Lucas let out a horrible scream and thrashed his body around, smacking away the gremlins as quickly as he could, but their claws were just too long, and their jaws were just too sturdy. They latched on, even as Lucas pulled himself to his knees and tore another one off, helping to rip the flesh off his arm after the gremlin refused to let go.

Lucas reached for his dresser, only to find another gremlin poised and ready. It pounced on him, targeting his upper lip. It dug its claws into his cheek to get a good hold on him and imitated the action of the first one, by tearing away the upper lip. Lucas howled with pain as he lost his footing and fell back to the ground. The gremlins swarmed on him and dug after his teeth. They tore through what little protection his gum provided and retrieved their rewards. Lucas was left with the remains of his face torn and tattered as a warm pool of blood soaked his head. He stared into the corner of the room.

The figure smiled back.

*　　　*　　　*

Lucas woke up.

The familiar horror creeping through his body, accompanied by an unfamiliar pain, brought Lucas to his senses as a scream ripped through his empty mouth. His hands clawed at the torn flesh surrounding what remained of his gums as his body contorted from the weight of the unbearable agony.

A timid little gremlin crawled from beneath the bed and darted out of the room and into the hallway beyond Lucas's awareness as he lay screaming on the floor. It kept its precious treasure securely buried in its paws and its pace even until it approached an outstretched, gloved hand. The gremlin approached cautiously before hesitantly placing the bloodied present in the exposed palm and was rewarded with a view.

The tall figure adorned in black faced the mirror with its free hand eagerly teasing the edge of the white mask. Once before the mirror, the mask slid up to expose grayed flesh that had fallen victim to time years ago. The flesh was rotted and stretched with the decomposition, becoming a mask of its own. The figure revealed its possession as a lonely, bloodied tooth, still dressed in a green bracket, as it held it up to the mirror. With a soft moan, its jaw fell open, letting the flesh covering its cheek tear as it unhinged its jaw, exposing several sharp teeth sporadically placed through its mouth. The figure gingerly held the tooth before the mirror and pushed the root of the tooth into its molded gums, while a black tongue slid beyond its lips in concentration. The figure leaned back from its reflection as its lips curled into a smile, cracking as it did and admired its appearance.

What a lucky find.

ANGEL OF MERCY

by Joseph Rubas

Joseph Rubas is the author of over 150 short
stories in the horror genre. His fiction has
previously appeared in: *The Horror Zine, The
Storyteller, Horror Bound Online,* and others. He
currently resides in Massachusetts with his
girlfriend, Brenda, who is also a writer.

Mark Hoffmann pulled into the parking lot at half past
three on the afternoon of June 13 and slid into a vacant
slot near the loading dock, which stood desolate and dust
swept. He killed the engine, shutting Sean Hannity off in
mid-sentence, and leaned back in the seat, a heavy sigh
building deep in his chest. He looked at his face in the
rearview mirror and let it out, stale, pent up breath. He
was scared, frightened out of his mind. His eyes were
bloodshot from lack of sleep, and his chin had begun to
darken with stubble. Usually he kept clean shaven, but
lately that didn't seem to matter.

Nothing mattered anymore. Mark took his trembling
hands off of the steering wheel and reached into the
glovebox. The snub nose revolver sat atop an overstuffed
envelope. He took it and stuck it into the waistband of his
scrub pants. He covered it with the hem of his top and got
out, glancing unconsciously around the still lot. Most of
the spaces were empty. He saw Happy's battered old Ford,
Tom's Mazda Miata, and a few other assorted vehicles
belonging to other staffers on other wings. The facility was
operating on the barest skeleton crew possible. Fewer and
fewer people were coming in every day.

Pushing the observation to the back of his mind, Mark
strode across the parking lot and bounded up the concrete

loading dock steps, his entire body tingling. He no longer felt safe outside. At the curb before his apartment earlier, he'd almost been taken from behind by a bloated, green-faced woman in a bloody hospital gown. If her foot hadn't scraped against the sidewalk, she would have gotten him. They had a way of sneaking up on you in the outdoors. It was their element.

At the door, Mark looked over his shoulder. The pavement ended at the base of a small, weed-snarled rise that flattened out into a long, brown field that fell away to the new high school, an uber-modern alter of brick and gleaming glass. Not a single living being was in sight, save for a few blackbirds soaring through the hazy heavens, and Mark couldn't even be sure if they were alive. If people and ground dwelling animals could reanimate, why not birds?

Mark slid his card in the slot, heard the familiar click, and pushed the steel door open, the stench of stale piss and disinfectant washing over him like a noxious wave. Before him lay a long, dim hall. At the end sat the nurse's station. Someone sat bent over something on the other side of it, and before them was a blurry figure in a wheelchair, most likely Mr. Jordan.

Mark pulled the door closed behind him and walked down the hall, his sneakered feet making no noise. As he got closer, he saw that the nurse at the post was Tom Walker, who, finally roused from his work, was looking up. Mr. Jordan offered an indifferent glance and went back to looking at his liver-spotted hands.

"Mark," Tom said, "glad you made it in."

Mark nodded. "Yeah, me too."

Tom chuckled. "You're crazier than a shithouse rat, Mark."

The nurse's station sat at a three-way intersection. Down either hall Mark saw only emptiness, except for Mrs. Avery, who shuffled like a zombie away from them, toward the double doors to B-wing, which had been abandoned at the beginning of the week as more and more residents either went home with their families or left on their own, if they could. For a moment, Mark couldn't tell if she was in fact alive or not.

"She's fine," Tom said, as though he had read Mark's mind. "She just came and got her pill a few minutes ago."

"Goddamn drug addict," Mr. Jordan grumbled bitterly without looking up. It was a known fact that she was, but who cared? It kept her calm and quiet.

"Wait until six 'o'clock," Tom said, once again focusing on ADLs. "You'll be asking for your fix."

"Go to hell, you fruit."

Tom sniggered. "I might be gay, but at least I can walk."

"Fuck you!" Mr. Jordan cried, and then wheeled himself away in a huff. Mark looked after him.

"Anything happen today?" he asked as he turned back to Tom.

"Ms. Johnson died at lunch. Just fell over on her tray and went. Me and Dean dragged her into the front office and cracked her skull open with a hammer."

Mark winced. Ms. Johnson was such a sweet old lady. She'd been really bad off since the beginning of April, talking out of her head and screaming at night, so he was fully prepared for her to go, but it was still a shame.

"Then we got a call from the company that brings in the food. They're closed. Our shipment was canceled."

Shit. "How much do we have in the kitchen?" he asked.

Tom shrugged. "Not much. Maybe a few days' worth."

"Oh no," Mark sighed. If the zombies didn't get the old people, starvation would.

"Yep." Mark looked up from his paperwork. "If I come in tomorrow I might bring in some cans mom has in the pantry. Nasty shit like chopped liver, but, hey, it's food."

Tom left at five after Stacy Simmons came in. He told Mark that he was willing to stay until seven if no one else came in, but after that he was gone. That would leave Mark alone with Doreen Marcus, the shift supervisor, and Ben Wright. The last of the kitchen staff had left after lunch, so Mark and Stacy had to make the food themselves.

After they had passed the trays out, they joined the others in the dayroom at the end of the building. The television, mounted in one of the corners, was playing CNN. Images of looted storefronts and riots in New York flashed across the screen.

"This is crazy," Doreen said with a shake of her head. She sat at one of the tables with a mug of coffee forgotten near her right hand.

"No shit," Happy laughed raspily. He usually hung around until midnight in case he was needed. He wasn't on the clock, but since his wife left him, he didn't have much to do anyway. "Only gonna get worse. I don't care what the gov'ment says."

"When are they supposed to evacuate the rest of the residents?" Mark asked as he sat down.

"Who knows?" Happy replied, "I doubt they even care."

A ball of despair formed in Mark's stomach. If the National Guard didn't come and get the rest, they were screwed. They were all too weak and sick to protect themselves, and it would be madness on his part, and the parts of everyone else, to stay.

"They said sometime this week," Ben offered. It was Thursday. That was unlikely.

***

It was midnight. The wing was dead quiet, save for the occasional groan or scream from one of the rooms along the darkened hall. Mark had filled out his ADLs early and sat trying to concentrate on a dog eared copy of the Free-Lance Star at the nurse's station, and each sound startled him so badly his heart slammed sickly against his chest. Nursing homes were always spooky in the late hours, but even more now. Any one of the residents could die and come back without anyone knowing it.

Mark was finishing an opinion article on the government's handling of the current crisis when the phone rang, scaring him into a scream.

Panting, he picked up the handset. "Heritage Hall, A-wing."

"Yes," said a hesitant female voice, "this is Amanda Haggerty. I won't be in tonight."

This was the third such call Mark had taken tonight. It looked like no one was coming in for the graveyard shift.

"Alright," Mark made a note, "stay safe."

"I'll try," Amanda Haggerty laughed humorlessly.

Mark hung up the phone and sighed. He would stay over, then.

The night passed in a sluggish blur. Mark restlessly roamed the halls, checking in on the residents and glancing out the windows in the dayroom. He was the only one on the floor, and he carried his gun openly.

At half past one, a call light winked on down at the end of the hall. Terrified of what he would find, Mark forced himself down the corridor. He hesitated at the door. It was dark inside. He reached his hand in and felt for the switch. When it came on, the room was flooded with cold white light.

There were two beds. Under the covers atop each lied a thin, emaciated old man. Between them sat a nightstand boasting a lamp and a telephone. The man closest to the window was hooked up to several machines, none of which Mark could name.

He was awake and frightened, his faded blue eyes wide and his mouth working feverishly. His fear infected Mark, who suddenly found himself wanting to bolt back to the nurse's station.

"What is it, Mr. Jones?" Mark stammered, taking a step into the room.

Mr. Jones shook his head and tried again to speak.

"Nightmare?"

Mr. Jones shook his head. "...Zombie..." he breathed.

No sooner had the words left his lips, something slammed into the window. Mark screamed and fell back. Mr. Jones started and let out a moan.

On the other side of the glass, a dead, gray face peered in. Its teeth gnashed with unholy hunger, and its eyes grew as it looked from Mark to Mr. Jones.

"It's okay," Mark panted, his heart racing. "I'll get it." But how? The thought of opening the door, even for a second, scared the shit out of him, and actually going out into the night, where any number of undead could be lurking, was out of the question. He couldn't do it. He just couldn't.

Mark inched toward the window. The zombie pounded anxiously on it and let out a long, low groan. "I'm going to open the window and shoot it, okay?"

Mr. Jones nodded, his eyes flickering to the gun in Mark's quaking hand. "Where....?"

"Bought it," Mark said, never taking his eyes off the zombie. He smiled as he approached. Dirty fucking thing.

Mark took a deep breath. Now the only thing separating him and it was a thin pane of glass. He licked his lips and raised the sash. The ghoul seemed shocked, and backed away. Though the government painted them as completely stupid, Mark didn't think they were. Not entirely. He saw one throw a rock at someone it was chasing. It didn't go far, of course, since the zombie was all screwed up, but the fact that it used a tool was petrifying.

After a dazed moment, the thing grinned and lurched forward. Mark fired twice, taking its head off its shoulders. The roar was deafening, and his ears rang for over a minute afterward.

He sat in the jerry chair near the window, and Mr. Jones watched him with something like terror.

"I shouldn't have done that," Mark said more to himself than to Mr. Jones. "More will come."

Mr. Jones nodded. His roommate hadn't even stirred. "Get some sleep," Mark said, and then got up and closed the window.

***

Two aides called in before daybreak, and a third just after sunrise. The only person who came in was Doreen.

"Am I it?" she asked him.

He nodded. "Unless they send someone from another wing over."

Doreen snorted. "That ain't gonna happen. I bet'cha ain't no one else come in either."

They had, Mark saw as he left, but not many. Only a few.

Going home, Mark came across four or five dozen zombies. His neighborhood was free and clear, though. A bunch of men in mossy oak camo stood around a huge pick-up truck, talking and laughing. They had banded together at the beginning and swore to protect their territory at all costs. They weren't doing such a bad job of if, either.

Mark pulled into the driveway and killed the engine. The house, a small ranch, was dark and empty; he was

72

inexplicably afraid to go in, afraid that a zombie would ambush him in a dark hallway.

Mark sighed, mustered what courage he could, and went inside.

***

Mark overslept and had to rush. The sun was sinking low when he pulled into the parking lot...which crawled with zombies.

He made three passes, honking his horn and circling the shuffling corpses, until Tom Walker came to the back door. "Who's in there?" Mark called as he slowed before the loading dock.

"Just me and Happy!" Tom called back.

"On the floor?"

"In the whole building!"

Tom's words struck Mark like a hammer, "What about the residents?"

"All here!"

Fuck! Mark looked over his shoulder. The zombies were closing in, their arms outstretched and their mouths chomping hungrily.

For a moment, he thought about driving away. It was hopeless. There was no way they could keep the zombies out much longer. Let Tom, Happy, and all the residents fend for themselves.

No. He shuddered as he saw images in his head of defenseless old men and women ripped apart in their beds, terrified and shrieking in agony. He couldn't live with himself knowing he'd run off and left them to die.

Instead of driving off to safety, he killed the engine, got out, and ran to his death.

"Come on!" Tom screamed, "hurry!"

Heart bursting against his ribcage, neck tingling as if expecting a sharp blow, Mark took the steps two at a time, and darted into the building ahead of Tom, who slammed the door behind them.

"Fuck!" Tom shouted, "they're all coming this way."

"Good!" Mark, bent at the waist, hands clasping his knees, panted. God, he was out of shape. "Maybe it'll...draw them away from the windows." The back door was heavy, the window narrow and crisscrossed with wire mesh. They'd never get in.

"I hope," Tom said, "but..."

"Who's that, Tommy-boy?" Happy called from the end of the hall, his voice echoing up and down the empty corridor.

"Me!" Mark called back.

"Mark?" Happy squinted, and then smiled. "How ya doin?" He came forward like a man to a long lost brother, a tall, thin redneck with a weather worn face and twinkling blue eyes. Mark noticed the shotgun slung over his shoulder, and felt slightly reassured.

"Been better, Happy," he said. The three of them now standing in an almost conspiratorial huddle.

"I hear you there. This is startin to suck."

Yeah, it was. They were pounding on the door now, dozens of cold, dead hands clapping in demonic rhythm. A woman cried out from her room, her voice high and petrified.

As if that one scream opened his ears, Mark heard soft weeping, moans, and wailed prayers. It sounded like hell, and it turned his stomach.

"So, we're it?"

"No one else came in," Tom said, his hands on his hips, "Doreen left after lunch and never came back. Then the DON on A-Wing left just before you got here."

Mark nodded. Thinking back, he was sure he'd passed her.

"We're all alone," Happy said.

Mark licked his lips, his heart beginning to race. "We have to call someone. The cops..."

"Already did," Tom said, "got a recording."

Fuck. "What about the National Guard? Maybe..."

"We done tried them too," Happy said sadly. "They said they'd try to get someone out, but they're busier 'an hell."

Mark sighed. He seriously doubted they'd ever seen any guardsmen. How many nursing homes were there in the state? A hundred? Two? They'd never be able to evacuate them all, even if they wanted to, which they probably didn't; a bunch of old people knocking on death's door probably weren't their top priority.

Mark closed his eyes. The pitiable sounds of terror threatened to shatter his soul. Someone (it sounded like Mr. Marsh in 6A, but he couldn't be sure,) screamed that something was at his window.

"Me and Tommy been tryin' to block off all the windows so those assholes can't get in," Happy said. "We got maybe three quarters of 'em done."

Mark looked over his shoulder at the door. There seemed to be fifty of them now, all crying out in their malignant bloodlust. "Alright. Let's do that first..."

"Wait a minute," Tom said. "I'm not staying here forever. It's almost dark, and the radio said night's when their most active."

"I wouldn't go out there if I was you," Happy said, "looks like they're plenty active to me."

Tom shot Happy a dirty look. "Yeah, imagine what midnight will look like. You think we can keep twenty-thousand of those things out? Hell no. They'll smash in here no problem, and we're fucked."

It was true. There were far too many windows in the facility; it was impossible to protect. Yet the alternative was much worse.

"You're fucked if you walk out that door," Mark said. "Look at them all. You think you can make it to your car without getting swarmed?"

Tom sighed. "I can try. At least I'll have a chance if I go now. You two should come with me."

Happy looked as appalled as Mark felt. "And leave all these old people to get torn apart? Man, I can't do that."

"Fuck them. Most of them are half dead anyway."

Righteous indignation flooded Mark's chest. How in the name of God could someone be so callous? Tom wasn't exactly the Patron Saint of Old People, but this...this was outrageous.

"You know what," Mark said, struggling to keep his sudden anger down, "if that's how you feel, just go, okay? I couldn't live with myself if I ran away and let these people die like that. Have you seen what those motherfuckers do to people?"

From the look on Tom's face, he had. Though the news networks censored the more violent content for broadcast,

Youtube, The Huffington Post, The Blaze, and countless other online venues showed the most gruesome footage in its entirety.

"I don't wanna end up like that," Tom said quietly, "and if I stay here, I will, and so will you."

The banging at the door had gotten louder, the moans more urgent. None of them spoke for a long time. Finally, Happy said, "I'm with Mark. You can go ahead if you want to, but I'm stayin'. Might as well. If we pull together and get this place in shape, we'll be fine. Got food, medicine, TVs. Rather be here than at my trailer. Probably torn apart already anyway."

Mark nodded. "Tom...please stay. At least for the night."

Tom bit his lip and looked over his shoulder. "Fine. But..."

"IT'S AT THE WINDOW!"

***

Happy was off like a shot, sprinting down the hallway with his rifle at the ready. Mark followed, and Tom brought of the rear, jogging halfheartedly.

The scream came from 5B. Mrs. Dandy was a short, white-haired former schoolteacher on dialysis. She had lived alone in the room since the previous summer, when Mrs. Myers, an old black preacher's wife, caught pneumonia and died. She rarely left her bed, but tonight she displayed as much energy as Lance Armstrong; Happy nearly collided with her as she ran out of the room. The look of terror on her was face heartbreaking, and Mark froze dead in his tracks. "Mrs. Dandy? Are you okay?"

The old woman, her hands trembling, collapsed pantingly against the wall, her cadaverous bosom heaving violently. "Mark," she stammered, "it was...it looked like..."

Glass shattered and Happy screamed. "Jesus Christ." Two resounding reports followed, filling the world. Tom, who was standing in the threshold, looked scared, and he backed up just as Happy flew out, slamming the door behind him. "Get the tools," he spat. Tom muttered something and rushed off toward the nurse's station at the head of the hall. He returned with a hefty toolbag. As Happy dug for something to block the door, Mark led Mrs.

Dandy down the hall to an empty wheelchair. The old woman sat but continued clutching his hand.

"Mark...what's going on?"

She didn't know, and that didn't surprise Mark one bit. Mrs. Dandy had begun losing her grip on reality several months ago, and she had been sliding irrevocably down ever since. She didn't watch television or read anymore. Most of the time, she sat in a corner, lost in memory. "That person looked dead."

Mark licked his lips again. "It's okay, don't worry about it. Happy's taking care of it right now."

She gave him a quizzical look. "Why don't you call the police?"

Mark forced a fake smile. "Good idea. You stay here."

Back up the hall, Happy had wrapped a heavy rope around the door handle and stretched it across the corridor, tying it to the doorknob of an empty room.

"What was it?" Mark asked as Happy stiffly stood.

"Zombies," Tom said. "When the window broke, three got in right off the bat. Behind them...oh, a hundred more."

Mark's heart sank. "That many?"

"Oh, yeah," Happy added.

"How many vacant rooms do we have?" Mark asked.

"Sixty, I think," Tom said.

The recession hadn't been kind to Heritage Hall. In fact, in the weeks before the dead began to walk, it had come really close to being closed down by corporate. Most of the residents had been moved to other facilities since 2011. Thank God in hindsight.

"What we need to do is get everyone on this floor and shut down the rest of the building. Don't worry about the empty rooms. Just close them off and board them up. Then..."

"You're forgetting something," Tom said, and before Mark could ask what it was, said, "a lotta the residents are on machines. If we take them off, they're dead."

Mark inwardly collapsed. He was right. There was no way. But there was also no way that the three of them alone could protect the entire building.

And if no one came soon and the power went off...

Things were looking bleaker all the time, and it was only just now dark.

"Then let's get to work."

***

They were done by a quarter of ten. Most of the windows in occupied rooms were boarded strongly enough, but toward the end they ran out of nails and had to evacuate a few residents from a different wing. Mr. Jordan and a few of the other male residents volunteered their services, and they had no other choice but to accept. Some of them were in near perfect health, and it was a shame that they were even here in the first place. Families, though, often discard their elder members for a number of reasons, sometimes greed, sometimes laziness.

By the time ten rolled around, Happy and Mark were passing out dinner while Tom handled meds (he wasn't licensed to; on a normal night, an RN would have done it). Most of the residents in their right minds had questions. Mark tried to answer them to the best of his ability, but had to lie more often than not; they all wanted to know when they were being rescued and by who, and Mark, unfortunately, didn't know.

When food and meds had been taken care of, Happy and Mark met Tom at the nurse's station. Tom, looking annoyed, cradled a phone between his ear and shoulder as he started, and then abandoned, ADL's. Finally, after a long moment, he slammed down the handset with a loud "Fuck!" and sat dejectedly back in his chair. "Now the guard office isn't even answering. We're fucked. That shit we put up isn't going to keep those things out."

"Tom," Mark reprimanded, "keep your voice down."

"Fuck you!" Tom shouted, standing up. "I shoulda left when I had the chance. You guys can kiss my ass." He stormed off toward B-Wing. Happy and Mark both called after him, but he didn't listen.

When he was gone, Happy and Mark looked at each other.

"You think he's leaving?" Mark asked.

Happy shook his head. "He's just gonna go piss and moan somewhere else. He'll be back."

Mark nodded. "Happy...do you think he's right, though? I mean, we can't keep them out for long."

"Maybe not. I think we have a shot, though." He stopped, seemed to think for a moment, and said, "what else can we do?"

***

They smashed through the windows and amassed in the halls, a legion of the undead, gray and rotting. Mark stood frozen as old people, old people he had come to love, were ripped to pieces. Helpless, they merely laid in their beds, screaming and crying, some of them calling for long dead husbands and children, and others wailing for help that would never come. Happy crouched behind the nurse's station and took about a dozen of them out before they overwhelmed him. Tom was trapped in a corner, swinging a hammer from Happy's bag. He got maybe three or four before one caught his arm and took a huge chunk out of his neck; hot blood spurted like a fountain at Busch Gardens.

Then it was only Mark. He was too scared to move, yet they were advancing on him, their mouths open and their eyes cold. The closet one...

***

Mark jerked awake with a scream, his stomach sour and silent tears streaming down his face. Someone screamed, and a shot went off. Fuck. Heart slamming, Mark jumped up and ran in the direction of the commotion, the B-Wing.

When Mark got there, he was horrified to see that his nightmare was becoming reality. Zombies filled the corridor, slowly shambling onward like an undead deluge. Happy stood about ten feet back from the hoard, shooting and screaming. Tom was wheeling an old woman away from the horror, while several elderly men escorted other woman after. Screams, high, primal, and painful, filled the hall. People were being ripped apart in their beds.

After a moment of horrified indecision, Mark ran into the nearest room, and found Mrs. Avery, who once worked for the Department of Defense back in the forties, lying dead in her bed, her face contorted in agony. Heart attack, it looked like. Natural causes regardless.

Back in the hall, he bumped into Happy. "Get outta here! There're too many!"

The undead advanced on. Helping a little old lady who stood dazed in the hall, Mark made it to the heavy steel doors to A-Wing. Happy slowly backed toward them, firing here and there, dropping zombies left and right. Mark remembered the revolver in his pocket, and pulled it out. He aimed at a zombie, fired, and hit it in the throat. It stumbled back and nearly tripped over an empty wheelchair. Shit. He aimed and fired again, this time it went down for good. Little help that was. A hundred more seemed to take its place. Happy dropped two more.

"Come on, hurry!" Mark screamed.

Happy, done playing Shootout at the OK Corral, broke and ran through the threshold; they closed the big double doors just as the dead reached them.

"This is bad," Mark said.

***

They lost one more wing that night, C. Of eighteen residents on it, only six made it out alive.

In the hour before dawn, Mark sat sourly in a corner, disliking his dark train of thought. The horrors of the night filled his head, and the excruciated screams of the dying residents echoed in the chambers of his soul. He thought of what it must have felt like to be defenseless in bed as the zombies lurched closer, moaning for blood, and shuddered. He thought of his own grandparents, and how much he had loved them, how he would have done anything to protect them from the agony of a cannibal death. He dozed at some point, for he dreamt of his grandmother during her last days, sick and delusional in bed. Only instead of choking on her own phlegm, she was pulled apart by a hoard of the undead while he looked helplessly on. When he woke, he was softly crying.

The sound of the dead was louder now than ever. There must have been more than a hundred of them at the doors and windows. A few of them clawed at the doors in the empty rooms. Despite the hellish din, most of the residents were asleep.

Light was beginning to color the eastern sky when Happy sat heavily next to him. Tom sat in a swivel chair at the desk, trying desperately to get in touch with someone, but the switchboards were jammed.

"What's on your mind, Marky-Mark?" he asked. "You look like you're thinking mighty hard over here."

So Mark told him, told everything. Tom overheard and looked at him slack jawed, the way a man would when he heard something particularly incredible. Happy's face grew more ashen as mark argued his case. When he was done, he lapsed back into dark silence.

"Mark, I don't think I can do that," Happy said after a long moment.

Tom remained speechless. Mark couldn't help but feel their hot gazes on him. He felt like a barbarian for even saying what he did, but deep in his soul, beneath the layers of social consciousness, on a primal level, he knew he was right.

"I couldn't live with myself," Happy was saying.

"It's better than letting them get eaten. How many died last night? How many were ripped apart? We can't keep them out much longer. Tom was right. We're fucked. I can't..." he paused as he voice grew shaky... "I can't imagine what...what it was like for them, and if I can keep the rest of them from dying the same death, I will."

No one spoke for a long time. In another empty room, glass shattered.

Mark blinked back a rush of hot tears. "I don't like it any more than you guys do, but it's so much better than..." he trailed off.

For nearly half an hour, they stewed in silence. Finally, Happy spoke. "I'm not doing it. You're right, but I just can't. If you wanna do it, do it."

Could he? Could he actually do it?

***

He killed the ones in their right minds first, the ones who would know what was happening. Mr. Jordan was first. He wept as he went from resident to resident like the grim reaper, spattering brains against the walls and floors, butchering the lambs of innocence. Happy and Tom stayed at the nurses' station, their eyes closed and their ears filled with the sound of death.

He saved Mr. Jordan for last. He was down by the vending machines, the back of his chair to the door; beyond the little wire-mesh window, zombies jostled for position, pressing their faces against the glass like eager children outside a candy shop.

Mr. Jordan sat tall in his chair. He was afraid, of that Mark was certain, but he refused to show it...much.

"Do it," he said, his Adam's apple bobbing, "just get it over with."

"I..." Mark started, but Mr. Jordan cut him off.

"Yeah, yeah, yeah, just hurry up and do it."

His tone stung Mark.

Mark raised the gun.

"I'm sorry," he said.

He fired.

***

Done with the coherent ones, Mark moved onto the ones with dementia and Alzheimer's. Some of them had been wakened by the blasts, their eyes muddled and distant. Each one took a shot to the head. When he was finished, he dropped the rifle and walked dazedly away, lost in grief.

He wandered the empty corridors in a trance, the gunshots still ringing in his head. At some point in the morning, he found himself in the break room, sitting in a corner and weeping in the dark. God, forgive me, he thought over and over, rocking back and forth.

During the long morning that followed, both Tom and Happy came to him and tried to comfort him, but he was ashamed of what he had done, and sent them away. Happy told him that he and Tom had had to close off three rooms because the dead broke in. "What you did was hard, man, and it looked bad, but it was right. I respect you. I couldn't have done it. They'd be zombie shit by now if it was me."

Had he done the right thing? Had he really?

That question haunted Mark the rest of his short life...

NIGHT DRIVE

by C. Inferno

C. Inferno is an author from New York state. She loves to travel and often stays in locations that are supposed to be haunted. Her love of travel and the paranormal come from her parents; they have encouraged her by involving her in ghost hunts, paranormal or supernatural investigations, and going through reports of paranormal and supernatural events.

Dana and Zeke were tired after the long night, and they were glad to take the McKinnon Road and have a nice drive back home. The back road was rarely used, and they were the only ones that seemed to be on it tonight. They both had to work late at Chuck's Barbeque, Zeke as a waiter and Dana as a hostess. They were tired, and they did not want to hear the sounds of the night traffic. Zeke was driving while Dana enjoyed the cool breeze that slipped in through the open window.

Zeke looked over to his girlfriend, her dark hair was softly moving with the breeze coming from the window, her eyes were closed, and she was listening to the soft music from the radio. He looked ahead of his car and he turned off the radio, making Dana open her lovely brown eyes and look at him.

"Dana, you remember the stories about this road?" Zeke asked with a smile.

Dana looked out the window to make sure of where they were. She could only see trees and the dirt road, but then she saw it. The burned willow tree, standing in front of the full moon; she knew exactly where they were. She knew exactly what stories that Zeke was asking about, stories that the people of the town liked to use to scare their kids.

"I remember them, about the phantom that scares people off the road," Dana said with a nod.

"Think we'll see him tonight?"

"I don't think he exists, but you never know." Dana said with a small yawn.

"Tired?" Zeke asked and she nodded silently.

"So tell me the original story." Zeke requested, and Dana sighed.

"Why? It's late, and we both know it by heart."

"It'll keep both of us awake, we might get a scare, and then we can go to bed."

"Fine," Dana agreed; she knew this was Zeke's way of asking her to just cuddle with him that night.

Dana turned off the radio and took a deep breath to calm her mind; she wanted to remember the story as correctly as she could. Zeke was almost shaking in anticipation for her to start the story that they had heard from childhood.

"Back in October of 1863, an old man had a cabin out by the burned willow tree. This old man was only known as Old McKinnon, he was a mean old man that was hated by everyone that knew him. Even his family hated him." Dana started the story. She sounded like she did when she read books to her nieces: completely in the story and oblivious to the real world.

"Old McKinnon had a daughter, Julia. She was a pretty girl, and her father beat her for that. He was tired of chasing men off and he was tired of her good looks. He would beat her with a stick, his belt, a whip, anything that he had at hand."

"Then it all changed one day," Zeke said with a smile, and Dana opened her eyes, neither of them noticed the ball of light behind their car that was floating in the middle of the road.

"Shut up and let me tell the story!" Dana told him with a smile before closing her eyes again.

"One day, Old McKinnon found Julia packing a basket with some of her clothes instead of doing her chores. He demanded to know what she was doing, and she said that she was leaving, that she was going to marry a young man in the town, and that she was never going to see her father or get beaten by him again. Julia also told him that she was taking his farm, all the land that he owned, and that as his only living child, it would have to go to her."

"But he didn't like that." Zeke said and Dana sighed, she would have to live with his interruptions.

"No, he didn't. He screamed that she would never have his farm or his land. He ran out of the house and bolted the door, locking Julia inside. He went out to the barn, and he got the matches that he had hidden there. Old McKinnon went to the big willow tree by the cabin and snapped off a small branch, and he set the leaves on fire. He threw it into the cabin, and his daughter was burned alive. The fire was out of control in seconds. The only reason that it did not burn everything to ash was a thunderstorm that had come from the mountains, but the fire still had a steep price." Dana said, she stopped for a moment to gather her thoughts before she finished the story.

"The cabin burned, didn't it?" Zeke asked, helping her get back into the story.

"Yes; the cabin burned down, the willow was burned, Julia had been killed by the fire, and Old McKinnon was killed by the people in town when they saw what he had done."

"The town dragged him back to town, tied to a horse's tail, and then they hanged him in the town square!" Zeke exclaimed excitedly.

"Yes," Dana said with a sigh as she opened her eyes. "They then took his body and burned it. He was never buried and the story is that Julia and her father's spirit combined to make the phantom that now kills on this road."

"Do you believe in that story?" Zeke asked.

"There is a record that McKinnon lived here, he killed his daughter, and that he was hanged. There are also records of the accidents but I don't think that it is a phantom."

"But phantoms are supposed to be able to change shape, like this one; phantoms are also stronger than normal ghosts, and they tend to be violent, like the stories of the phantom."

"Zeke." Dana said, her tone told him to drop the talk of ghosts and phantoms or he was sleeping on the couch.

"You hear what people are blaming for that motorcycle crash last week?"

"Any sort of crash on this road is blamed on the phantom, who probably doesn't exist," Dana said looking up at the stars.

"Why would the authorities do that unless they believed the phantom to be real?"

"Because they would not have to investigate the accident, it is a scapegoat. Now drop it." Dana said as she rubbed her head, she could feel the migraine forming behind her eyes.

"Your meds are in the glove box." Zeke told her before he noticed something behind them.

"What the hell is that?" Zeke questioned as a light shined on them from behind.

Dana looked in the side mirror and could only see the light, nothing else. It almost looked like the headlights of a car except this was only one huge light. Dana and Zeke were confused since this road was rarely used because of the number of car crashes and accidents. The accident from last week had ended with the death of four bikers. That should have kept most people away from the road for at least a week. Dana felt a shiver go up and down her spine; there was something strange about this light and it scared her.

"Zeke, if this is a trick, I'm going to kill you," Dana warned her boyfriend, but Zeke only shook his head in silence.

The light started to come closer and closer, coming at their car faster and faster. Zeke sped up as he tried to put some distance between their car and this strange light. Dana turned in her seat to get a better look at the light as it got closer and brighter. Dana could only gasp when she saw what was in the light.

In the light, there was a old man, but he could not have been normal. The man was in what looked like an old miner's outfit, and he was running after the car. Bis skin was pale, and it looked like he was on fire. He was keeping up with the car, which was impossible since he was only running. Then Dana realized that she could see through the man. She could see the trees that lined the road and the few road signs. There was no way that it could be a trick.

"What the hell is it?" Zeke yelled, knowing that it could not be a car, since there was no roar of an engine.

Zeke sat up in the driver's seat, trying to peer through the rearview mirror and stay on the road. Dana put her hand on his arm, trying to get him to focus on the road, she did not want him to going through the thick trees or crashing the car. Zeke let her watch the miner, and he turned back to the road, taking quick looks in the side mirror to try to make out the figure.

"Nothing human," Dana whispered, her voice shaking as she watched the man in the light.

The man seemed to know that she was watching because he grinned, his mouth twisting into a smile and showing sharp, crooked teeth. Then he started to change. The miner's outfit changed and billowed out, the uniform turned into an old dress of rags and the man's face changed; his wrinkles smoothed out, his nose became smaller and his lips became fuller. The man was a woman now, but Dana and Zeke were still scared, and it kept chasing them.

"Fuck, it's the phantom!" Zeke yelled, he slammed his foot on the gas, making the car speed up even more.

Dana squealed in surprise when she was forced to turn around by her seatbelt constricting over her chest, she could only see the trees as a blur, and she could barely see the road in front of them. Zeke was going too fast for her to make out any details of the road or the trees around them. Dana's whole body was shaking as she turned around again to see what the phantom was doing now.

The phantom was not the woman any longer; instead there was a large horse with red eyes that galloped after the car. There was a man riding the horse, and in one hand he had an axe. Dana gasped and turned back in her seat, too afraid to see what it would turn into next. Then the light was gone.

"Where is it?" Zeke yelled as the car started to drift off the road.

"Zeke! Stay on the road!" Dana told him, and he swerved back onto the road.

Dana turned around to try to find the phantom but saw nothing.

"It's gone." She said in awe.

"What? Where is it? Where did it go?" asked Zeke and he turned around to see where the phantom went.

"Zeke, look out!" Dana yelled when she turned back in her seat and saw the car start to go off the road.

"Shit!" Zeke said, turning back to the road but then he yelled in surprise.

The phantom as the horse and rider stood before them, his axe raised high over his head as they ran through him with the car and then went off the road and down the hill. Zeke yelled as he tried to regain control of the car, but it kept rolling over the ground and rocks until it ran towards a tree. Dana screamed as they hit the tree, and it all went black when she hit the dashboard. Zeke went head first into the steering wheel. They were out cold and did not notice the gas leak or when it started to burn and flames engulfed the car.

The phantom horse snorted, and the rider just nodded at the two burning bodies in the car, before the two phantoms turned and faded away with each step the horse took. Dana and Zeke were just the latest in a long line of victims to fall for the phantom's tricks. The phantom just had to wait for a new victim or two to come on his road.

ENCOUNTER IN THE DEAD OF NIGHT...

by Sergio Palumbo

Sergio Palumbo is an Italian public servant/author who graduated from Law School and is working in the public real estate branch. His works and short stories in both the horror and sci-fi genres have been published in numerous magazines and anthologies worldwide. He is also a scale modeler who enjoys science fiction and real space models.

Hubert silently opened the rolling shutter, then jumped over the windowsill thanks to a furtive move and stole into the house. He very nearly lost his balance and almost stumbled over a bedside table positioned next to the left wall, but he finally got over it and simply went on.

He had a specific mission to accomplish this night!

The gloves the young Romanian man (only thirty-years-old) had on kept hidden the complexion of his skin and protected him from the freezing temperatures of the streets outside, at the same time making him feel more self-confident and unyielding. He had taken all the precautions needed, as he always did. He wore his usual belt with the typical housebreaker's tools and all the things he thought necessary. Moreover, his black outfit let him merge perfectly with the night that ruled everything by then, hiding his long pale blonde-hair. He had his knife, his rope, and a small flashlight that was going to gloriously enlighten the way towards his final end. Nothing could go wrong for him today! His mission would be successful this time, as with all the other times! His hands started fondling the pointed blade of the knife and then he put it at his slender waist. Yeah, nothing was going to go wrong...

He had started watching the lonely house a few weeks ago. A two-story cottage endowed with a wide garden and a small car parked out back. It was perfect for his deeds. He had gotten the detailed plans of the house, thanks to some acquaintances of his at the Cadastral Survey within the Bureau of Land Management, and he had inquired about the owners and their behavior - everything which could turn out to be useful, as usual. The man didn't like taking chances; it wasn't his way of doing things, certainly. Every step required the right care, the right time in order to be studied and examined thoroughly. To complete his task and reach his final target, he had to be ready for anything at any time, and he had proved to be ready, indeed, since that first day when he had cast his chestnut eyes on a calm, small family living in a village lost in the countryside that surrounded the outskirts of his hometown. Something had clicked on in his head, as if a sort of switch had been thrown that had been dormant for a long time before being finally activated. He was unable to hold out against such a tormenting, tempting voice at that time, and so he had acted hurriedly, almost by instinct, driven because of a fire started inside his mind. He was still young back then and came short of his aim at perfection that he would develop later with the passing of years, even though during that action he had already shown himself up to the job to be done.

Yeah, that one had been his first mission, the first murder he had completed, and his first duty! His recollections, however, seemed confused about such an action, and he wasn't too proud to remind himself of the several missed steps, as if his hurried work of that day was filled with embarrassment and mistakes, and so the event had many difficulties in finding its role and the correct place among his past experiences. That memory looked like something ingenuous and shabby that was unable to be fully recognized and considered as a real work of art by the artist, who was giving his best today. That was how as he was used to doing things nowadays. In fact, the feeling he had inside about that first time of his was imprecise and defective, just like a sort of discomfort, after all. The man had clearly improved a lot since then. At present, he had come to a serious perfection whenever he acted like this, and a very long trail of blood had accompanied his night hunting before today. Dozens of killings, many families wiped completely out while being inside their houses, without any explanation, deaths that just seemed to be incomprehensible and horrific before everyone's eyes, evidently – except before his own, of course. He had a senseless fierceness that left common men horrified, along with the policemen, and devastated everyone that had the opportunity to discover such a cruelty, anyway.

Weak people, limited persons, and inferior individuals! If only they could see visions the same as he was allowed to, if only they could watch the reality as clearly as he himself was able to!

After all, his missions were very easy: Hubert had to find the right subjects, chosen among the thousands that lived in one of the nearest towns of his homeland, then learn all he could about them and finally enter their homes in order to make them notice him, listen to him and eventually be instructed about, 'the way of light'. Then, yeah, just afterward, he had to complete his job and purify their souls, by lacerating their mortal remains... Everything was done so that others could know and comprehend, looking forward to their own moment!

Yeah, yeah, it was easy, and he was a master of that cruel art.

The place he had chosen this time was typical of his pattern: a small house drowned in the silent greenish surroundings, only a few neighbors around, all of them a bit reserved, frequently out of town on weekends; a family lacking in troubles, with two sons and lots of acreage for their belongings, and all the tools for gardening, too. The young assassin had always wanted to enter their lives, since the day he had seen them by chance for the first time. Soon, very soon, he could finally satisfy his desires, accomplish his task! The knife was already trembling with joy in his hands...

He crossed the open space past the window he had crawled through and got to the main drawing room. There, before him, he could see directly to the wooden flight of steps climbing upstairs. In a few minutes, he was eventually going to put an end to all the voices tormenting his dreams, to fulfill the will of his unknown masters that controlled and inspired all of his actions day by day. That is, he would soon be showing his new, unwilling followers the true light!

He began going to the second floor, slowly, silently, paying attention not to make a single noise. The long flight of stairs went on inexorably, and he was approaching, approaching, and approaching more and more incessantly.

The pointed blade of his knife seemed to have its own life so far; it moved and wriggled among his long fingers, as if it felt that the target was near. The luminous beam of his flashlight opened the way ahead of him. Before his attentive eyes, a short path stretched and, in the end, he was able to see two doors. It was the last one, the farthest and the bigger one that led to the bedroom of the adults, the one he had to face at once, immediately, if he wanted his work to reach its conclusion. He would take care of the sons later on, the light was going to reach them, too, but only afterward...

Suddenly, Hubert thought he had heard a movement nearby. He stopped and kept listening carefully for some time. Nothing....

Maybe he had only imagined it, who knows? Yeah, it had to be just so! The assassin stared at the metal he had in his hand and proceeded with caution, switching off the small lamp. Then he approached the decorated door that guarded the bedroom and put his fingers on the golden handle. "Hurry up, hurry up!" he told himself. "The voices can't let go of me, the masters can't wait any longer!" The weapon seemed to be whispering in his ear. "Quickly, show them the light!"

The door passively opened forward, revealing a wide, expensively decorated room. His eyes darted around quickly, examining everything. "Wait a moment, how come...?" He thought suddenly, to his great surprise. There was something going on that was no good at all! An irritating, freezing wind was coming from the window on the other side of the room and lightly touched his face. The man looked at that and noticed that the shutters were completely open. They weren't supposed to be that way! Why? Maybe he hadn't been attentive enough this time, maybe he hadn't been watching the routines of those homeowners closely enough, it might even be that...

A strange movement next to the long bed drew his attention to it. What was that? Was it possible that someone had already awakened...? Immediately he switched his flashlight on again and pointed the beam towards the source of the unusual sound he was hearing. As soon as the ray of light hit the target, a monstrous scene appeared in front of him. At an end of the double bed, his head bowed over the neck of one of the two spouses, who looked to be innocently asleep, a very slender and almost awkward individual stood, his paleness similar to a corpse's - making the young man shudder at first glance. His very long, pointed fingers ended in horrible nails, and the head displayed sores and pocks half-hidden under the rare black locks. The picture was horrific this way, but that just wasn't all! The incredible, unnatural being -- be he a monster or something else -- had his mouth touching the skin of the unconscious male body lying on the bed. The husband didn't make a single move but had on his face a desperate look while those two canine teeth, much longer than the assassin had ever seen before, were deeply sinking into the jugular vein of the unfortunate, slowly draining all of his life energies out in superhuman way. Some blood trickles were dripping sideways, profusely and vividly.

It was just a sight too, awful even for Hubert. The man soon dropped his flashlight and stood still, unable to do anything, looking forward to his destiny to come. Wasn't it funny, after all? The most famous, ill-reputed serial killer in the whole country, Hubert himself, was meeting by chance that night the King of all the serial killers along his path. And he was to give in to him, of course...

He could have fought, resisting and trying to kill him. What about jumping on him with force, piercing his unearthly whitish body using his knife, more and more, deeper and deeper, or just turning and running away, attempting a very hard escape from that place? But he knew all of that was going to prove useless. A sort of hypnotic call was already keeping him right in place, undoing his own will and making fun of the young man as if he was only a lost baby. Killing him? "What an absurd thought!" Hubert told himself. How could he ever harm that superior being, a very strong creature, the final assassin that was continuing without a break in his foul action?

Hubert's voice already proved too weak to get out of his mouth, stuck in his breathless throat, while his arms were dangling at his side. The man dropped his knife to the ground, too, leaving aside the blade that had been his trustworthy fellow over the course of so many missions of purification, always accomplished previously.

Now a new voice was taking the place of those many calls his mind had been listening to since he was a young boy, but this time it seemed to be different, stronger, irresistible, and sweeping. The young assassin was told to surrender, to passively give up, and to wait for him. No, he couldn't do anything at all, absolutely! Just watch and wait for his turn in there.

The man felt he was entering another person's hunting ground, in a way. 'Ubi mair minor cessat', the old Latin saying went, that is: 'where there is the major, the minor becomes negligible'. He knew it very well, there was no other way!

Another noise came ahead of him, another movement of the creature. Yes, sure, now his time had come. No more missions similar to the many tasks he had completed before, no more exciting runs at night, and, of course, no more opportunities to show the others the light. Today, it was his moment, he was going to learn the lesson, to know a new reality and enter another world of sufferings. So, while that monstrous being was coming nearer, his canine teeth approaching his neck, Hubert had no doubt that it was going to be hard for himself.

And very painful.

KITTENS WITH CHAINSAWS
by Johannes Pinter

Johannes Pinter is a Swedish movie director and horror writer. He has directed two feature films (of one, *Sleepwalker*, the remake rights have been sold to Hollywood), and has written one horror novel (currently unpublished, but pending) and an assortment of horror short stories, some of which have been published in a Swedish horror anthology.

Stig "Styx" Lundgren knows how to twist a story, and he knows that they know; they, being his readers, the critics, the juries.

It took a couple of books before he found his winning formula; horror mixed with Scandinavian crime, a hefty dose of social criticism and human drama. Six books all totaled sold over two million copies in Sweden alone. Paperback editions not included. Everything translated into twenty languages. The Glass Key for best crime and two time Pocket Prize winner. And on the wall in his study, the most prestigious trophy of them all: the framed letter from Stephen King that confirmed what he already knew; that he has one hell of a twisted mind.

Not bad for a small town kid with nightmares.

Stig secretly thinks that he owes everything to them, the nightmares that he had when he was still Stig. That was of course before he became Styx the horror author, channeling all his darkness into his fiction. In interviews he sometime jokes that he went from living with nightmares to living his dreams.

The shaved head (which he conveniently introduced when his hairline started crawling too far north), the braided beard, and the tattoo of the ferryman Charon in the neck all played their part to reinforce the image of the guy who is buddy with man's darker side.

But perhaps his "Styx" persona would get dented if people could see him now, zinc tub in his arms, trudging across the lawn from the small red painted cabin with white corners, dressed in moss green fleece shirt and rubber boots.

The cell phone rings. "SONYA" the display says. Stig presses the green button and wedges it under his chin, so that he can open the door to the crumbling shed that crouches under the spruces.

"Hi, honey," he says as he puts the zinc tub on the floor.

"Hello. How you doing? You seem okay", replies Sonya.

"Was down to the lake earlier. I've got the grill ready and maybe throw on a chop later."

Stig adjusts the tub.

"Not jealous," Sonya says jealously. "When we retire, I'll come too. Don't wanna be trapped here in this stuffy editorial forever."

"Mmm."

Stig's not amused by the idea of having his wife around when he's out here working. He's here to escape life, to focus on what's important in life, without having to play social games.

"You staying the weekend?"

"Probably. Final adjustments take time. Maybe I'll close everything if I get the...."

"Don't! I want a reason to come out once more before winter!"

"Okay." He waits. "Anything else?"

"No, no. Just wanted to hear your voice. See you Sunday night. "

"Definitely. Love you."

"Back at ya."

Stig puts the cell on the workbench.

It's only 3 pm, but the light streaming through the dusty window fades as the sun sets behind the dense spruce forest. He turns on the light, and the small shed's interior turns yellow. Gardening tools. Skewed garden furniture. A broken scooter. A wooden hammock with a torn roof. Chainsaw, ax, and pruning saw in a corner and the workbench with its tool wall.

Stig absently strokes his bald head, which feels stubbly after a few days without a shave. He hesitates, then goes for the elongated shape of the half round ring file.

He sits on his haunches and adjusts the zinc tub once more, ensuring that it is located correctly under the cat wretch that is hung upside down in a rope from a hook in the ceiling.

It's a dapple-grey European Shorthair. Probably calling its home the farmstead a mile and a half through the woods. It has duct tape wrapped around its little head. Stig always carefully shuts the mouth, but lets the nose be uncovered. It must be able to breathe. Live as long as Stig wants it to live. It's the screams he wants to keep away. The sound of cats screaming is so awful. Enough pain and they scream like an injured child and that Stig doesn't like!

The cat is hung by its hind legs, a rope tied around each paw. Then a stick is attached between them, keeping the legs spread.

Stig looks into the cat's yellow eyes. It looks stressed out. The thin pupils steadily staring into Stig's pale blue eyes. It tries to struggle but it's not easy when its forelimbs and tail are taped to the body. What an ugly little piece of shit, helpless and sickening. Stig hates it!

Then he feels it: the long-awaited wave of heat pulsating through him. When the primal instincts takes place where the superego has just ruled. When it's finally okay to turn off his brain, and let the bestial impulses take control.

He grasps the cat's body with his left hand while placing the narrow end of the file against the cat's anus.

"Here comes hell..."

With full force, he rams the jagged metal rod into the soft hole. The cat's thin body immediately starts to cramp with pain.

***

With a wet smack, the remains of the little animal's body lands in the blood-stained tub. Stig looks at the massacred limbs. The ring file did an efficient job with the soft parts. Then he placed it in the vise, and with great patience he broke every bone, limb by limb, of the still twitching body. When he was finished, the cat had just been like a skin sack full of sticks and gooey mess. It had screamed. All the time, from the first second, it had screamed, continuously and in unimaginable pain. Stig knows that it did although it could hardly be heard behind the thick layers of duct tape.

Stig puts the gardening gloves on and throws the remains in a plastic bag. He takes the shovel behind the shed door and strolls across the lawn past the large birch. He kicks a plastic ball and enters the woods behind the cabin.

If he walks ten minutes, he reaches a place that neither Sonya nor the twins would even think of visiting. It's a chaotic maze of dense spruce forest, sprawling dead branches and fallen trunks.

The highest and mightiest tree in the forest is his landmark. Reaching it, he pats it a couple of times; he wants to treat it well so that it doesn't reveal his secret. Then he lifts the moss between the roots and digs into the already thoroughly worked-through soil. Sweat barely breaks before he hits a black plastic surface.

Soon he uncovers the pile of "business" from recent years: about twenty sacks, each containing the remains of missing cats.

It wouldn't do to have Sonya around when he works. She wouldn't appreciate her husband's therapy work in the shed. Finishing his books is just one goal of Stig's solitary stay. The second - the unofficial goal - is to get the darkness out that no therapist in the world could reach.

Until five years ago, the dark nightmares fueled his creativity. But when life is wrapped in too many layers of fluffy cotton, the darkness fades. Then you need something new to feed the fire. That was when he began with the cats ...

Stig throws the bag down in the hole, shovels dirt over it, and finishes by placing the covering of moss over everything.

On the way back, he walks past the hill. He stuffs the gloves into his pocket and, leaning against the shovel, takes a deep breath of the clear autumn air. Looking down towards the lake of sparkling water between the trees, he hears nothing but the wind whispering in the tree tops. It is so quiet and peaceful out here. Each time is like the first time. After a few weeks he usually likes to go back to Stockholm, but like this, with short intense periods, it's like heaven. It always has been since he was a kid. Despite all his money, he has never even thought about switching Myrberg to something more modern.

Stig's feeling great. The new book will kick ass. He just knows it.

***

In the evening, while he adjusts chapter 37, Stig hears the thunder for the first time. Rain clouds gathered as he ate the second dish of tortellini while sitting in the wicker chair on the patio. Now, he stands by the window watching big drops of rain run like little transparent snakes down the glass. A dull rumble sounds, followed by a flash of light. He counts to five Mississippi. Five kilometers.

Stig completes the chapter, brushes his teeth, and then settles with a well worn copy of Kings Night Shift. He's always liked to delay sleeping when it rains. He can lie for hours and read and hear the soft patter of raindrops on the roof.

Thunder is followed by lightning. Two Mississippi. Stig finishes the story. Snuffing candles at half past eleven, he falls asleep almost immediately.

***

BOOM! Lightning and thunder at exactly same time.

When Stig comes to his senses, he has somehow already jumped out of bed, dazed and staring. It takes a couple of seconds before he can orient himself as he stands swaying in the darkness. Man, he had such a horrible dream. He tries to remember but cannot. When that static discharge lit up the world, it extinguished the images in the dark parts of his brain.

He pulls on a pair of sweatpants and a t-shirt and goes out onto the patio. Standing under the patio roof, he sees through the rain the highest tree in the forest on fire. The lightning struck in his spruce. He hopes it will not become a problem. He sees the rain dampening the flames, keeping them under control. Stig gasps. What would it have looked like if the fire department arrived and have stepped right into a cat mass grave? Would he have been punished for it? How many years does one get for cat killings? Stig grins. Note to self: check cat grave tomorrow.

He walks inside and closes the door. He goes through the combined living room and kitchen. The moon finds a gap in the clouds and casts a light beam through the room. His laptop rests powered down on the coffee table next to three empty bottles of Staropramen and a nearly empty plastic bowl of barbecue potato chips. He passes the stairs to the upper floor and walks into the small bathroom.

He doesn't bother to close the door when he stands straddled over the toilet seat and pulls down his sweatpants. He relaxes and with an exhalation lets the remains of the Staropramen stream into the bowl.

A faint clinking sound causes him to pinch off the flow, as his whole body tightens in sudden preparedness. What was that? Was that glass that broke? He listens hard and, with great difficulty, tries to squeeze out the last drops. As he reaches out to flush the toilet, he hears the sound of movement in the living room that is immediately drowned in the toilet's deafening flushing sound. Damn, why did he push the button? Stig, irritated, tries to discern any sound through the heavy noise from the toilet.

He flinches as he hears a drawer in the kitchen fall to the floor. No mistaking what that was as he quite clearly hears forks and spoons spreading over the kitchen floor. And knives.

Now Stig is starting to get scared. Someone is in the house with him. Someone is taking great liberties with his possessions.

He looks around the mosaic bathroom for something to defend himself with, some kind of weapon, maybe his toothbrush, or a soap on a rope handle in the shower corner. He chooses the toilet brush mainly because of its length.

He stands with his back to the wall, toilet brush high and feeling immensely silly. However, the alternative, to not hold anything at all, is somehow even worse.

"Hello?" he shouts carefully. No response of course.

He stands still and listens. When the toilet's tank is refilled with water, everything is finally silent again. Stig hears shuffling from various sources out there in the room. Sounds like animals. Rats? They have never had rats here. He saw a dead wood mouse once (in the mouth of a cat whose head he then cut off with a blunt bow saw) but that doesn't count. Probably animals seeking shelter from the rain and made it into the house. It is probably not a human anyway.

Then Stig feels the wave of heat surge in his body again. This is not a dangerous situation. He is in control here! Its' a few small animals. What can they do to him? This is, in fact, a new variation of a familiar scenario: Stig versus a small animal. Just that now it will not end with one animal. He will catch as many as he can. Then, one by one, they will bitterly regret that they invaded his territory. Perhaps it may even inspire a new novel, at least a short story. There's not enough intrigue in that setup to fill 350 pages.

Stig sneaks out of the bathroom, into the living room. In front of him, he hears the sound of small paws padding over the wooden floor. He puts aside the toilet brush and grabs a broom. Damn critters. They will regret that they-

Stig howls in pain and surprise when he feels a sharp sting in the back of the calf. He whirls around, waving randomly with the broom. He sees a hairy something disappear behind the couch.

He feels with his hand. The sweat pant leg is wet. Stig tries to light the floor lamp by the sofa without success. While looking around, he limps over to the wall button, but nothing happens when he presses it either. The power must've gone.

He feels the leg again. Damn it hurts! What the heck was it that stabbed him? Claws?

By the stove, he finds a lighter. Its flame provides enough light for him to see the pant leg has a red patch of blood. Stig is furious. These damn animals aren't going to hurt him in his own home! Constantly, he hears the soft scratching sound of paws over the floor, always on the far side of things in the room.

He takes a pot from the stove and throws it across the room. With a blaring sound it bounces over the armchair, splattering tortellini-leftovers across the room. Sonya will not appreciate the cheese sauce on the Ralph Lauren curtains. To his great satisfaction, it creates chaos in the darkness; soft bodies scattering in different directions.

With his eyes wandering the room's darkness, his left hand fumbles for another saucepan. Then something strikes his hand.

Turning his head, it takes a second before he realizes that he sees a cat. It looks as if it has rolled in the mud before entering. The animal is dirty and matted with soil and black ... blood? Its body is broken and warped, but despite all the damage, it stands up on its hind legs and has just pinned Stig's hand to the cutting board with a large meat knife. It takes a few moments before the synapses in Stig's body connect with the terrible pain of having a knife driven through his hand. But then he gets it, and he screams! He drops the broom and screams madly from the horrible pain.

Intense padding and scratching makes him turn his head. Immediately, he forgets that it hurts, and he stops screaming. The sight of an attacking horde of twisted, mutilated, burnt, bloody, armed cats is overwhelming.

If only for a second.

Stig sees he needs to get moving. Whimpering from the pain, he draws out the butcher knife that is stuck between the middle and ring finger bones in his left hand and is free. He slashes with the knife, cutting the closest cat in half so its entrails splash over the floor. Cat number two, a white Javanese armed with a fish knife, cuts halfway through of the muscle that controls Stig's right thumb. Cursing, Stig loses his weapon. A European Shorthair clings to his back, raises a pair of scissors and furiously begins to cut bloody tears in Stig's neck.

Stig roars. Grabs the cat and throws it to the wall with a dull thud but five other animals are on him. Knives, sharp glass shards and a steak fork are repeatedly stabbing Stig's legs, not so deeply but with high frequency.

Paralyzed with pain, he drops to his knees. The animals throwing themselves at him are now focused on his torso. Stig responds by sweeping his arm, throwing all the cats through the room. The clatter of soft bodies and metallic items is heard over the living room floor.

Stig looks to the front door, noticing that it is already half ajar. In the opening he sees the silhouettes of new cats come stumbling on broken legs and stumps, weapons raised and ready to attack.

Looking wildly around, he spies the coffee table and his laptop. Normally, he puts the laptop back in its cover. Why not yesterday? His new book is there and only there. A partial backup is on a hard drive at home, but it's not nearly as good as the current version.

Stig kicks aside two cats armed with chisels and hammers, reaching for the computer on the coffee table. It almost slips out of his bloodied hands.

The cats from the kitchen surround him. A Manx without eyes and ears attacks clumsily with a cleaver. Stig reflexively lifts his laptop and blocks the strike, lunging through the horde and up the stairs to the upper floor.

***

Stig shuts the bedroom door and locks it with the key. He quickly searches the small room with rustic wallpaper and a sloping roof. Except for the bed, there's only one painted white armchair and a low dresser.

Moaning, he sits on the unmade bed, puts the laptop next to him. Stig almost faints when he peeks under his clothes and sees all the wounds and tears that crisscross over his legs and hips. He just wants to collapse on the bed and drift away from it all. How the hell did this happen? While he shreds the pillowcase to put on the worst wounds, he feverishly tries to piece it together. All the cats are so deformed and mutilated and broken, but with such supernatural power. Are they some kind of cat army that has been called to his house to avenge all the cats that he tortured and killed over the years? It can't be his cats, come back from the dead, could it? Is there even anything like cat zombies? He's never heard of it. Well, in King's Pet Cemetery it was, but there was some hocus pocus involved, and it was just a book.

Absently, he sees if the laptop is okay while he thinks things over. It was great work, a meticulous work, he did with his cats. They are dead, efficiently and ruthlessly executed after he made their bodies unusable. Most of them should already be turned to dirt and now they're here, if they are here. But of course they're here! He only needs to look at his body to be reminded that they're here. Not only that, they're like Jason Voorhees cats. How the hell did that happen? If only he could-

The mobile phone! Why didn't he think of that? He can call Sonya, or 911. Of course! It is not on the bedside table. He gets up, limps over to his jacket hanging on a hook and feels the pockets. Nothing.

Pants and shirt are in a heap on the floor. He kneels and throws the clothes away. There it is. The Smartphone is nailed to the floor with a five-inch nail right through the touch screen. Stig closes his eyes and swears quietly. Someone must have done it.

He looks around. Too late. The meat club hits him right in the forehead.

***

Lying on his back, half way immersed in a pleasant numbness, he hears the pattering of small paws over by the locked door, claws that climb the wooden surface, the click of the door key, followed by the creaking of hinges when the door slowly opens.

Stig dizzily turns his head. He sees a shaggy Persian pushing the door open with his front paws. Its head polished; ears, eyelids and nose completely grinded away. Stig giggles like a drunk at the poor cat, it looks like a tiny wig stand. In his mushy brain, a crystal clear thought lights: it is definitely his cats that have come back. This little fellow helped him to test the new grinder a year ago.

The smile stiffens when he hears paws - many paws - coming up the stairs. Stig forces himself onto his elbow and manages to get on his knees before the first cat rallies through the door. It attacks with a letter knife, ramming it straight into Stig's right side. He groans, pushing away the attacker and getting to his feet. Six cats organize a common assault, throwing their bloody, filthy bodies against him, making him lose his balance. A utility knife rips through the air, cuts a deep wound in his right thigh muscle.

Stig drops to all fours on the bloody and sticky wooden floor. A whining sound is heard very close. He turns his head and sees a maroon Burma with a hollowed trunk raise a grinder towards him.

Stig's brain explodes with unreasonable pain when the spinning blade plows a deep wound along his left side. Muscles and tendons are torn without resistance as the spinning blade grinds a deep cut into his ribs.

Stig shakes and rattles and screams uncontrollably, just wants to get away from the pain. He turns, knocking the cat with the grinder with his elbow but more animals are already over him. It feels like a hundred fangs are pressed into him from all angles as he half lies on the floor. Something is driving a screwdriver into his right buttock. The dirty shovel from the shed falls like a broad axe inches from his nose, hitting the floor, cutting off two fingers of his left hand. The vengeful cat bastards have really found every toy in the toy box.

Making a last, valiant attempt, he raises his mutilated hand to the bed but doesn't have the strength to continue. A great weariness falls over him.

The bed is so soft and comfortable. If he could only lie there and rest for a while.

***

This is where he and Sonya made the twins. They've made love many times in it, both before and after they hit the jackpot with two healthy sperms that simultaneously crossed the finish line. The first time was twenty-seven years ago, when Sonya came for a visit when they first got together. They were nineteen years old. Stig's parents still owned the cottage. They had fucked like rabbits then, constantly and everywhere, of course also here. There was something special about that first time. He had never had a girl in this bed. It feels good that it was Sonya who was the first. Yes, it is definitely good.

***

Then he sees a dapple-grey European Shorthair, just inches from his tired, bloodshot eyes. It is shapeless, like a sack full of dough. Almost like that "Barbapapa" character from the children's book, Stig thinks. It moves strangely, floppy-like. He recognizes it; it's his last victim, the afternoon playmate. Stig crushed all the bones in its body, but nevertheless it manages to hold the blade of a sickle.

Before Stig has time to understand how a leather bag full of guts and bones can move, it chops, buries the blade tip in Stig's left eye.

He feels how something sticky wet runs down his cheek when the cat pulls out the blade and aims for a new strike. Stig is about to go crazy. But there's no time to pray or cry if he's to save his other eye. He hits the Barbapapa zombie cat with his decimated fist so that it loses the weapon and wobbles away over the floor. Stig takes the sickle and with furious anger, he slashes with it in all directions. He's not used to see with just one eye, so the attacks are a bit wild, but he does the job. Cat after cat is cut into halves and quarters, and soon Stig no longer feels any weapons piercing his body. He gets to his feet and stomps the spine of one cat, bashing another so that it burst like a piñata. He kicks a Persian so that it rolls away through the puddles of blood.

Pain and the loss of blood have left his body weak and now, just seeing with one eye is making him dizzy. He doesn't notice the bolt cutter until it's too late. With a distinct cut, two cats working together cut Stig's left Achilles tendon.

The foot immediately bends when the heel is no longer fixed to the calf muscle. Stig staggers and falls to the inner wall. He manages to grab hold of the window sill and just remain standing.

It hurts! It hurts so fucking much!

Kneeling, he looks with a watery eye out at the rain. In the darkness, beyond his own reflection, he gets a glimpse of the deep blue Opel Zafira parked on the lawn.

He looks around. The cats have mobilized and new weapons have arrived. It's now or never. With the sickle Stig hacks through the glass. As ten cats jump on him, he throws himself through the window.

***

The fall is about four meters. In healthy condition, he might have been able to calculate the landing better. But now he lands with the mutilated left leg first. It receives the full weight. The ankle is cut straight off, and the knee bends so that the lower leg stands in ninety degrees straight out in the wrong direction.

Stig screams like he's never ever screamed before. He screams so hard it feels like his throat is one big bleeding wound. His leg, throat and one hundred puncture wounds are competing as cause for the most pain, but Stig is currently in no condition to judge which of them wins. He can only scream, but there's no one to hear.

As the rain whips him, he begins to crawl towards the car, left foot trailing like a bag of meat behind. But he doesn't feel anything anymore. It is as if the body has turned off. Left hand, right hand, right leg. Left hand, right hand, right leg. Somewhere he finds the rhythm, just as the critics who tend to praise him for the rhythm of his prose. It's in the blood, baby.

He hears the cats at the front door. They are not so quick with their injured bodies and heavy weapons. Stig looks around, doubtful that he will reach to the car in time.

Then he sees the barbecue stuff he prepared earlier. After a few seconds of ambivalence he instead steers his mangled body toward the grill.

As the cats come stumbling over the grass with wet shiny metal weapons, Stig overturns the grill. With trembling hands he rakes the bottle of lightning fluid and firelighters. With blood slippery fingers he fumbles the cap off the bottle. The cats are almost there when he aims the bottle and let the first spray of lighter fluid shoot out and drown the little beasts. He then tries to push the lighter's trigger.

The first cat, a Scottish Fold, reaches and cuts his arm before the lighter's flame is lit. Stig puts the flame to the liquid jet as he pumps it over the attackers. The squirting liquid becomes a hellish flame that instantly makes all the animals burn like torches.

"Burn you bastards! Burn!"

Stig screams as he continues to spray fire until the bottle is completely empty. He looks at the burning cats. How they move in aimless circles in vain to escape the fire, until they collapse in charred lumps. He has sent them back to whatever hell they came from.

Stig collapses flat on the grass, closes his eyes and lets the rain wash him clean of blood and filth and insanity. Then he feels the pain again.

He gets up on his knees and start crawling towards the car again, Left hand, right hand, right leg, Left hand, right hand, right leg, until he is finally able to open the car door and crawl up into the dry leather seat. He opens the glove compartment and gets the car keys he always keeps in the unlocked car. Out here there are no intruders. Well, not until now.

He sticks the key in the ignition and starts the car. Looking at his hanging left foot, he's happy he drives an automatic. He adjusts the rearview mirror and looks into his own eyes. It's a madman's gaze, a person who's beyond all senses - but a person who is alive!

For the first time he feels secure. He will make it! He survived! He's a fucking survivor! Despite the pain, he pounds his fists on the steering wheel, in the ceiling, and on the dashboard as he yells in triumph! They thought they'd get him, but he had a surprise ending for them that they hadn't counted on! He is the fucking king of twists!

He releases the hand brake, puts the reverse gear in, and starts rolling backwards out of the gate. He enjoys the thought that the next time he stops is at a hospital where they make damaged bodies whole again.

Then he hears an engine start somewhere. It's hard to hear where the sound comes from through the rain and what it is. But it's way too close. Is it a scooter?

Stig doesn't react, or think, or even lift his foot off the pedal, when the windshield is shattered into a million pieces.

The last thing he sees is swirling fur and gleaming yellow eyes before the roaring chainsaw cuts him in half.

EVEN THE GREAT WILL FALL

by Thomas M. Malafarina

Thomas (www.ThomasMMalafarina.com) is an
author of horror fiction from Berks County,
Pennsylvania. To date, he has published four horror
novels; *Ninety-Nine Souls, Burn Phone, Eye Contact,*
and *Fallen Stones,* as well as five collections of
horror short stories; *Thirteen Nasty Endings, Gallery
Of Horror, Malafarina Maleficarum Vol. 1,
Malafarina Maleficarum Vol. 2,* and most recently
Ghost Shadows. He has also published a book of
often strange single panel cartoons called *Yes I
Smelled It Too; Cartoons For The Slightly Off Center.*
All of his books have been published through
Sunbury Press. (www.Sunburypress.com). He is the
curator responsible for content selection of this
anthology.

In addition, many of Thomas's works have
appeared in dozens of short story Anthologies and
e-magazines. Some have also been produced and
presented for internet podcasts as well. Thomas is
best known for the twists and surprises in his
stories and his descriptive, often gory passages have
given him the reputation of being one who paints
with words. Thomas is also an artist, musician,
singer, and songwriter.

His arm, the one in which he held the hunting knife,
flew back reflexively and to his extreme relief, John felt the
blade sink deep into the cushiony flesh of the pursuing
thing's repugnant, decomposing face. He tried to withdraw
it while simultaneously running for his life, but his hand,
now covered with the puss-like, viscous substance, oozing
from inside the creature's wound, slid from the handle as

the beast crumbled to the floor, leaving the blade sunk deep inside its skull and lost to him forever.

He could hear them; what sounded like dozens of them now only a few feet behind him and he could also see the open door just up ahead. That room, whatever it might be, would have to be his sanctuary; at least he hoped it would serve as such, even if only for a brief time, perhaps just long enough for him to come up with a plan. The door grew closer, only a few inches away, but just as he placed his right hand on the knob he felt something grab onto his left shoulder.

Once again, reacting with the skills he had been taught, his left elbow shot up and back with lightning speed at what he correctly assumed was the appropriate height. He was rewarded with the satisfying feel of cartilage shattering under the impact of his blow, and he heard a guttural moan as the creature's nose was apparently obliterated and its many tiny broken bone fragments were driven upward into the thing's putrefying brain, immediately destroying whatever it was that allowed the foul abomination to still be walking the earth.

As John backed quickly into the small room and slammed the wood-paneled door closed behind him, yet another one of the rotting beings thrust its hand between the door and the jam. Its decaying fingers with segments of yellowed bone visible in places where the skin had rotted away were instantly severed by the impact of the closing door. The digits fell to the floor where they continued to wiggle like mindless worms for a few seconds before blessedly going still.

John stood gasping, trying desperately to catch his breath, his heart thudding maniacally, feeling as if it might explode inside his chest. The air in the room was pungent not only with the stench of them, the creatures on the other side of the door, but also from something inside the tiny room itself. Looking about John immediately saw the room he had chosen for his temporary refuge was a small bathroom.

Glancing up at the ceiling John estimated the room to be about seven feet wide by ten feet long. At floor level, most of that space was taken up by a toilet, a vanity, sink and a shower stall area. Since there was no longer any electricity anywhere in the world, the only light available came from a small window located a foot or two above the toilet.

John's hopes that the window might provide a means of escape were dashed when he saw how small the opening was. Even in his thin and starved condition, the window was far too small to allow him to crawl through, and although he was unfamiliar with the building or this particular apartment, he was fairly certain he was on either the third or fourth floor. He had lost count as he had been running for his life up the dark interior stairway. Even if he was able to fit through the tiny window, the fall to the ground might kill him, or even worse, it might cause him to break a leg, and then he would never be able to outrun them.

He decided instead to look around the room and see what he could find to help him. He had to use his training. He had paid a lot of money to be trained how to survive, and as such, he was supposed to have gained the necessary knowledge for just this situation.

John lifted the lid of the toilet seat and was revolted to find it filled to the brim with human waste, both solid and liquid. With the contents exposed to the air, the stench became overpowering. He let the lid fall shut and leaned against the side wall, holding back the bile which was working its way up from his practically empty stomach. He hadn't eaten in days and couldn't afford to lose whatever little nutrition still remained. The door to the bathroom rattled as one or more of them slammed there fetid fists against its panels and clawed like a pack of rats trying to get in; to get to him. John understood time was of the essence.

The best thing for him to do was to focus on what his mentor, Sam "Sergeant" Steele had taught him. Sam Steele was the former Special Forces soldier and multi-degreed black belt who had instructed John's survival class. John had taken the class on a whim, never believing he might actually need it. The first thing Steele had told the class was that at a time of crisis, they should always keep their cool and use their cunning and intellect to find a way out of trouble.

One thing Steele had stressed repeatedly during their sessions was that when everything fell apart and the world was thrust in to chaos, "even the great will fall". It was one of his favorite sayings. By that, John assumed he meant that no matter how big, how strong, or how well prepared someone might be, even the best of the best could slip up and could fail. Steele taught John and his fellow survival students to use their wits to resolve any deadly situation they might encounter.

"Almost anything can be turned into a weapon for self-defense" the sergeant had always said. "Just use your ingenuity and commons sense to figure out how to find and use whatever is available to create weapons to guarantee your survival."

John knew now was the time to put the sergeant's teaching into action. Although it was almost impossible for him to concentrate with the ungodly stench of the confined space combined with the steady pounding on the door and the horrible grunts and scratching of the undead creatures beyond it, he did his best in order to determine what he might use to defend himself.

He understood that sooner or later, he would have to go back out there among them. He had few other alternatives. He could stay in the foul smelling stinking hot bathroom and eventually starve to death, or he could kill himself. Neither of those options was any more appealing than trying to fight his way out. "Even the great will fall." He heard the voice of Sergeant Steele say again in his head.

John reluctantly approached the vile toilet once again and removed the porcelain lid from the water tank on the back of the unit. It felt heavy and solid, and although a bit unwieldy, it might make a good head-bashing weapon. He reached inside the back of the tank and removed a long copper rod which supported the ball-cock flushing device; this toilet's flushing days were long gone. He had to work it back and forth a few times until it eventually broke off at the handle. Connected to the arm was a small chain used to lift up the rubber water release stopper. Both the arm and the chain might prove useful to him.

Just above the small bathroom window over the toilet hung a tattered curtain. John reached up and pulled down the thin, sharp curtain rod. It was one of those two-section types made of light gage metal, with ninety degree bends on one end of each side used to attach the rod to the wall mounted fixtures. He removed the tattered curtain from the rod and set the two parts of the rod along with the toilet tank parts on the filthy linoleum floor. The steady banging and scratching continued on the other side of the door.

Then he noticed several thin, gnarled fingers creeping through the one inch space at the bottom of the door. One of the creatures was apparently trying to reach under the door; perhaps to gain leverage to pull the door open – as if they possessed such intelligence - or more likely, the thing was just trying to reach underneath in a futile attempt to grab him. John picked up one of the two parts of the curtain rod and, using the right-angle side like a handle, drove the sharp end down on one of the fingers, severing it cleanly. The flimsy rod bent and John's hand slid along its edge resulting in a small laceration on his palm.

The creature withdrew the remainder of its fingerless appendage from under the door, leaving behind a snail trail of some greenish-black fluid. A few drops of John's own blood dripped on the floor near the opening at the bottom of the door. The creatures on the other side must have smelled the scent of fresh blood because they began to bang against the door even more desperately as if working themselves into a state of frenzy.

He wiped the palm of his hand on his filthy jeans and examined the wound, happy to discover it was not deep and would not need to be stitched. He would have to clean the cut somehow soon if he hoped to avoid infection. In the world as it presently existed, an infected cut could be fatal.

"More." John said with frantic desperation. "I need to find more weapons; something besides these few crappy things." He threw the now worthless broken curtain rod against the door, causing a fresh round of groans and scratching from the creatures on the other side.

John went to the wall mounted medicine cabinet but found nothing inside of much use, save for a collection of expired prescription drugs, which he supposed he could use if he ever decided to kill himself. He had no idea what they were, but he was certain that swallowing all of them might possibly be fatal.

"Maybe not," he said, slamming the cabinet door with frustration. He knew he could never kill himself, no matter how much he thought about it, not unless he had no other alternative and unless he could make certain he would not come back as one of those horrible things. He did manage to find a bottle of hydrogen peroxide however, which he quickly used to clean out his cut. He would worry about finding some way to bandage it later.

On top of the vanity below the medicine cabinet, he found a pair of six-inch long stainless steel hair trimming scissors sticking out of a wicker basket along with a hair pick equipped with five long metal pointed rods extending out from the handle. These would most certainly come in handy albeit just for the sort of up close and personal self-defense he was hoping to avoid. The pounding on the six panel door continued as the thin pieces between the cross members began to vibrate with each subsequent impact, looking as though they might not hold out much longer.

John imagined the famous scene from Stanley Kubrick's adaption of Steven King's "The Shining" where Jack Nicholson breaks through a similar door with an axe, sticks his face through the opening, and says with his trademark Nicholson grin, "Here's Johnny." He knew when whatever was on the other side of his door finally broke through, there would be no clever tag lines spoken, just growls, grunts, and a savage desire to rip his insides out.

He next opened the two doors on the base cabinet of the vanity and began frantically looking for other helpful items. He found a can of hairspray, which still seemed to be quite full. He wished he could have found a cigarette lighter. He thought he had read somewhere once that the contents of a pressurized can of hairspray could be potentially flammable. Maybe that was urban legend, maybe not. But, if he could find a lighter he might be able to test it out by devising a makeshift flame thrower.

But there was no lighter anywhere. Apparently whoever lived last in this apartment was a non-smoker. John thought, "Looks like all that healthy living didn't do very much good once the dead started roaming the streets."

There was little else of any defensive value inside the cabinet except for something which he was very happy to find. For some reason, someone had left a full roll of duct tape in the cabinet, and as any do-it-yourselfer or survivalist will tell you, duct tape can most certainly be your best friend. Score one for the good guys. John also found a spare roll of toilet paper and fashioned a makeshift bandage for his hand, which he coated in peroxide and wrapped with some of the duct tape.

The rest of the stuff inside was just shampoos and conditioners and other such hair care products. Perhaps if John had some knowledge of chemistry, he might be able to concoct something dangerous from the various ingredients, but he didn't, so he closed the doors in frustration.

God! The place smelled disgusting! And John suspected it was not just the stench from the overflowing toilet which was accosting his senses, but something else; because there was a much more rank and rotten stink lurking just below the foul reek of fermenting human excrement.

He turned around and examined the shower curtain and its rod which was mounted high above his head. "Yes" John thought with great satisfaction. It was apparent that the rod was not one of those flimsy thin-walled types you often found in home centers; the kind which was nothing more than a frail tube of metal plated with brass or chrome or sometimes coated with a colorful, decorative plastic. No sir-ee, this baby looked to be old school. John was certain it was constructed from actual, heavy-gauge, galvanized piping; not much for fashion or design, but strong and reliable. This meant it would most definitely serve as a good weapon, not just to shove into their slack-jawed mouths and up into their rotting brains, but also to be used as a club to cave in as many skulls as possible. His martial arts training had included bow staff technique, and this rod would fit the bill perfectly.

John reached up and grabbed the left side of the rod, jerking and pulling on the pipe with all of his might, trying desperately to rip it from its wall anchor. When it finally did let loose, John fell backward landing butt-first against the cracked Formica top of the vanity with a painful jolt. The right side of the rod then fell from its holder, crashing to the floor, as a buzzing swarm of thousands of blue-black flies rose up and surrounded John's head. He swatted frantically at the air around him scattering the pests in all directions and dropping his side of the curtain rod to the floor with a metallic clang. When the swarm finally dissipated, John's breath caught in his throat at the sight before him; the reason for the revolting swarm of flies.

Someone, probably the former inhabitant of the apartment, was sitting in the tub, leaning against the back wall. At first, John feared the horrid mess might be one of them waiting to take him down, but then he realized what he saw could no longer do him or anyone any harm, and he also understood at once where the other foul stench had been coming from. It was from the fetid, stinking mess of putrefying humanity, which was all that remained of the decomposing body in the tub.

The cause of death was apparent by the shot gun lying against the thing's chest. The barrel was pointing up toward a place where the thing's head should have been, its skeletal finger still locked around the trigger. John reached out to retrieve the shotgun from the rotting body's clenched fingers. He tugged carefully but it wouldn't budge. Files flew about the remains angrily. John knew he would have to tear the gun free and likely sever the corpse's fingers in the process. Then he realized he was simply not up for such a task. His stomach was already on the verge of vomiting and would only need a little persuasion to push it over the edge. He simply could not bring himself to do it. He convinced himself the shotgun was likely empty anyway, as the owner would have only loaded enough shells to do the job.

Besides, he already had a hand gun of his own tucked into his pants near the small of his back, but that was as useless as the shotgun would surely be, because it too had no bullets. If those creatures broke through the door too soon, perhaps he could bring himself to quickly rip the gun from the cadaver's grasp and use it as a club, perhaps not.

But either way, the gun was going to stay where it was for the time being.

As John reluctantly studied the corpse, he saw a strangely interesting pattern of brown and gray fragments of flesh and gore stippling the back wall, resembling some twisted, horrific work of bizarre modern art. The stump of the body's neck was infested with larvae and insects. The front of the hideous cadaver's formerly grey tee shirt was dark with congealed blood. John could tell it had once likely been a man. The queasy feeling began to return with a vengeance, but John still could not take his eyes from the horrifying sight.

The flies had now returned to their task of laying eggs in the rotting corpse. What appeared to be hundreds of holes had been bored in the bloated body's decomposing flesh as maggots made their way freely beneath the mottled skin, which throbbed disgustingly as their bodies squirmed about. John was now barely able to control his urge to vomit. Then he saw a particularly large insect, a worm of some sort slithering just below the flesh of the body's headless neck, resembling the pulsations of a vein in the throat of a living person. John could no longer hold back his retch.

John vomited what little still remained in his stomach into the bathtub, coating the corpse and shot gun with the vile fluid and disturbing the swarms of flies once again. As he heaved uncontrollably, he felt some of the wretched insects trying to fly inside his mouth. This only served to nauseate him even further as he puked and spat out a mixture of bile and still moving insects.

He managed to fall back away from the horrid scene, sitting down on the floor with a thud, unable to support his own weakened body as he leaned his back against the doors of the vanity and stared without really seeing at the mess of what had once been a living human being. He realized he would never bother retrieving the shotgun now.

Since the plague had started, John had seen many sights no man should have to endure, and he truly believed he had seen just about every vile thing imaginable. However, the condition of the maggot-infested carcass in the shower had taken revulsion to a new, previously inconceivable level.

John suddenly felt as frighteningly unprepared for what awaited on the other side of the bathroom door than he had ever been in his life. For the first time ever, John was starting to question his own sanity. After all, what sane man would want to survive in such a world as now existed? Suicide was likely a saner act than attempting to go on living.

"Oh for Christ's sake, just suck it up!" John heard a voice shout in his befuddled mind. "Who... who was that?" he heard himself say aloud. Then he realized he recognized the voice in his mind for what it actually was; the voice was that of Sergeant Steele. Then he recalled Steele telling his class in his patented snarling sergeant's voice, "When the airborne defecation hits the rotating ventilation people, even the great will fall. But not you... not my students... you people... you will survive... because dammit, that's what I've trained you to do!"

But John still had his doubts. He knew there were likely dozens of those ungodly things out there, and he was on his own. If it were true that even the great had fallen, what chance could he possibly expect to have? Then he remembered his training, and, getting up from the floor and dusting himself off, John prepared to go to war as he had been taught by his mentor so many months ago.

He lifted his end of the heavy shower curtain rod and let the curtain fall back into the tub, covering the hideous cadaver. Then he began to fashion his arsenal of weapons from the various items he had found in the bathroom. As he did, he was worried he might not finish in time as the thin panels of the door seemed to be bulging inward under the constant scratching and pounding pressure of the creatures beyond.

First, John took the remaining half of the thin metal curtain rod and, using the roll of duct tape, he wrapped the L-shaped end of the rod to protect his hand from any more cuts and forced the metal piece he had taken from the toilet tank, down through the center of the curtain rod to reinforce it and give it a bit more strength, securing it also with duct tape. He realized the chain at the end of the metal tank arm was too short and too flimsy to do him any good, so he wrapped that and taped it to the rod as well to keep it out of his way.

The six inch scissors he had found were tucked into his back right pocket to be used only as a last resort in the event of close-combat. He put the hair pic with its metal tines into his left back pocket. His hand brushed across his empty hand gun, and he was reminded of the shotgun in the hands of that rotting body and once again found himself fighting the urge to vomit. He closed his eyes for a moment and regained his composure.

Then he went back to work, taking another piece of duct tape and securing it to one side of the can of hairspray with plans to pull it over the top of the push down aerosol button and tape it to the other side when the need arose to provide a constant stream of spray. Even though it might only be a momentary diversion, it could provide him with the second or two he needed to survive.

The toilet tank lid would be one of the first weapons he would use when the creatures broke through the door. Next, he hoped to use then the heavy shower curtain rod, although it was too long to use properly in the close confines of the small bathroom. He was certain when he was out in the main room, this would become his weapon of choice. As such, John wrapped the middle section of the rod with duct tape to give himself a more secure surface for gripping the weapon. He did the same thing with one side of the heavy toilet tank lid, as its surface was far to smooth to have any natural gripping capability.

John put the remainder of the roll of duct tape into his jacket pocket for future use, assuming he still had a future, and prepared himself to face the enemy. The curtain rod now leaned against the outside wall of the shower where he could quickly grab it when he was ready. He didn't exactly have a plan, but he did have the start of a strategy which he hoped would save his life.

He set the toilet tank top and the can of hairspray on the vanity then grabbed the sharp window curtain rod by its now protected taped handle and stood silently staring and the ever weakening door as the undead creatures began breaking through the thin wooden panels. Slivers of wood splintered as boney fingers worked their way through the newly made openings. John recalled the words of Sergeant Steele telling his class to remain calm despite the desire to panic in such situations and to keep their heads clear.

"You won't have the luxury of being scared, people. You cannot panic. You don't want to run around like a bunch of chickens with your damn fool heads cut off. You will be strong, you will remain calm, and you must think, think, think people!"

John had no idea how many times he had heard the sergeant repeat those and other similar mantras. He drilled his ideas into the psyche of his students until they became second nature; not so much a thought as a reflex, and luckily for John, that was exactly what happened to him.

Dead fingers began to tear the door panel to bits, and not so unlike the image he had imagined earlier of Jack Nicholson, one of the horrid creatures put its face against the opening, its one dead eye looking into the bathroom directly at John with a savage and wanton hunger. Its other eye was missing, leaving a maggot-riddled blackened orifice which oozed some brackish dark green fluid. Without a moment's hesitation, John pressed the thin, reinforced rod deep into the creature's exposed remaining eyeball and up into its brain. The thing let out a mournful cry and fell backward, collapsing. John could see several others, perhaps three of four of them milling about outside the door, looking down at their fallen comrade but obviously not comprehending what had just happened to him.

John took advantage of the creatures' moment of confusion to make his move. Grabbing the bathroom door handle he pulled it quickly inward. One of the creatures must have been holding onto the handle on the other side because his rapid motion caused the beast to fall into the room landing face first on the floor in front of him. As the creature started to get up, John grabbed the toilet tank lid and brought it down hard on the top of the creature's skull, caving it in amid a flying flurry of flesh, skull fragments, brain matter and gore. The creature went limp at his feet.

Another one of the things started to step over the corpse of the first in an attempt to get at John. Thinking quickly, John grabbed the can of hairspray and, securing it in the shooting position with the duct tape, he blasted it directly into the oncoming creature's eyes. It let out a cry of anger or perhaps pain, John didn't care which, and while the thing was distracted, he brought the toilet tank lid down on its head, shattering its skull and breaking the lid into several fragments as well, rendering them both useless. Then he saw his chance to escape.

Three of the creatures remained outside in the other room and were several feet from the doorway. John grabbed the heavy shower curtain pipe and ran into the room with all the speed he could muster, holding the rod out in front of him horizontally. One of the creatures was caught in the throat and its neck was broken, severing its spinal cord and destroying it instantly. A second one made a clumsy lunge for John, and using the pipe like a bow staff, John struck it with several rapid-fire blows that dazed the creature enough for him to swing a final head crushing bash.

He quickly spun the pipe, and as the final creature made his attack, John thrust the rod forward, into the thing's gaping mouth and up into its maggot-infested brain. It fell to the floor with a thud. John tried to pull the pipe from the reeking carcass but discovered it was stuck. He supposed had he been willing to take the time, he might have eventually worked it loose, but he decided it was better to cut his losses and get out of the place as quickly as possible and find a new safe house to hide in.

John slowly approached the door leading out of the bedroom and was surprised to find the living room of the apartment free of creatures as well. Now he just had to make it out into the hall which would give him access to the rest of the building or to the outside if he so desired. He was lucky; the hall was empty.

Creeping stealthily down the hallway, John kept his eyes and ears open for more of the horrid things while trying unsuccessfully to find another open apartment door. As he turned the corner, he stopped in his tracks, his breath catching in his throat. There were at least ten of the wretched beasts huddled around the disemboweled corpse of some poor soul that they had cornered in the corridor and had overpowered. John realized they had not yet noticed him. He thanked all that might still be considered holy in this atrocious hell on earth and slowly backed away from the scene of wanton butchery.

After a few feet, John was about to turn around when he felt himself back into something. He stood stock still and could hear a faint wheezing followed by a guttural growl coming from behind him, starting low like the gentle rumble of a motor but slowly growing in volume and sounding more ominous by the second. John knew without looking just what was waiting behind him, and he hoped he was lucky enough that there might only be one of them.

Reacting at once, John simultaneously reached into his left pocket and retrieved the hair pick with the metal-pronged handle, while sinking down, spinning and bringing up his right arm with the intention of getting it around the creatures head. If he did the move exactly as he had been taught, and at the same time swept with his right foot, he would bring the creature down while his left hand came up with the hair pick and pierced the creature's eyeball and brain.

The move went perfectly, except his aim was slightly off and the pick sunk into the thing's cheek, which didn't serve to do anything but anger it further. The undead thing lay on the floor of the hall on its back grabbing pathetically at the comb still sticking out of its face. That was when time seemed to come to an abrupt halt for John.

What he saw shocked him to the very core of his being. This creature was not just another one of those unnamed walking meat sacks; this was one he recognized. He couldn't believe his eyes. It was... but how could it possibly be? It was Sam Sergeant Steele, his survival coach, now reduced to a brainless bag of rotting flesh. John thought to himself "Oh my God! Sam was right. Even the great have fallen."

The Sam creature started to get up for another attack, but before it could, John reached into his right back pocket and withdrew the six-inch scissors. Without a moment's hesitation he sunk the tip of the scissors deep into the gray-filmed eye socket of his former mentor, pushed it up, up into its brain, and watched his former friend go limp, falling back to the floor with a thud.

John quickly rose to his feet, sprinted down the hall away from the carnage, and suddenly found himself outside once again. There fortunately were none of the horrible creatures anywhere in sight, and John was able to make a safe getaway, guaranteeing his survival for at least one more day. He had no idea how long he would be able to subsist in this horrifying new world, and he understood he would have to measure his existence one day at a time, but he knew with the training he had received from the man he had just put down, he might actually last longer than he imagined. As he walked away, John took one last look back at the building he had just left, said "Thanks Sam," as his voice caught in his throat, and his eyes welled with tears. Then he headed down the alley, always alert and always vigilant.

HANDSOME JACK

by C.M. Saunders

C.M. Saunders began writing in 1997, his early fiction appearing in several small-press titles and anthologies. His first book, *Into the Dragon's Lair – A Supernatural History of Wales*, was published in 2003. After graduating with a degree in journalism from Southampton Solent University, he worked extensively in the freelance market, contributing to numerous international publications. Since returning to dark fiction, he has had stories published in numerous magazines and several anthologies. His novellas, *Dead of Night* and *Apartment 14F: An Oriental Ghost Story*, are available now on Damnation Books, while 2012 sees the release of his latest, *Devil's Island*, on Rainstorm Press. His literary fiction novel, *Rainbow's End*, is out now on Flarefront Publications.

"So do you really believe in ghosts?" It was Rhys who finally threw the question out there, undoubtedly giving his companion, Steve, more than a twinge of satisfaction at having held out for so long. It seemed like a valid thing to ask. This was, after all, an impromptu vigil in a supposedly haunted pub.

Steve had probably been anticipating such a remark since the moment the chubby landlord had wished them a good night and waltzed off into the bitter winter chill. There had been plenty of time to think up a suitably impressive answer. "The existence of the paranormal cannot be disputed," he began, his eyebrows rising slightly. "The real question is not whether or not ghosts exist, but why they exist."

Rhys rolled his eyes and groaned inwardly as Steve grasped with both hands this latest opportunity to show off his supposed knowledge and belittle one of his peers in the process. After all these years, the pattern was getting a little boring, but Rhys bit his tongue as Steve powered on. "That said, I do believe there is a perfectly reasonable scientific explanation for just about everything, even such crazy things as aliens and ghosts. We just don't know what that explanation is yet. The truth is people are not nearly as clever as we like to think. We can split the atom, big deal. We can walk on the moon, but we don't even know what lurks at the bottom of the ocean." Steve paused for maximum emphasis, studying his friend's eyes as if to gauge the effect of his infinite wisdom. He was just about to deliver what he thought would be the killer line when the uncomfortable silence he had so lovingly created was broken by a loud, searing scratch that seemed to come from all around them at once; the sound of fingernails being drawn agonizingly over wood.

The blood drained from Steve's face and his mouth formed a loose 'O.' "What was that?" he said.

Rhys stood and peered into the semi-darkness that surrounded them. He could see nothing unusual. His mind was cast back to what the chubby landlord had said earlier that evening...

***

"Oh, yes. Definitely something strange going on here, there is," the exasperated landlord told them. "Wouldn't like to guess what, but lately there's been all sorts of goings on. Weird sounds, mostly. That's how it seems to start."

Rhys stole a glance at Steve. They had known each other for so long that very often, no words were necessary between them. The landlord wasn't pulling their legs. He was telling the truth, or at least he believed he was. Sincerity was evident in his pallid, drained complexion, his furtive, darting eyes, and his nervous, fidgety manner. He carried with him the air of a man at the absolute end of his tether. He kept flicking stray strands of black, greasy hair out of his eyes, and he stank of Jack Daniels whisky. That was no surprise. He had sunk two double measures in the short time that Rhys and Steve had been present in the bar, courtesy of a couple inquisitive minds and suitably deep pockets.

"What kind of weird sounds do you hear?" Steve asked Les, the chubby landlord. He had always been the more out-going on the two, his life an endless search for excitement. In any given situation, he was the one asking the most questions, pushing the envelope wherever possible.

The landlord thought for a moment then replied, "Thumps, mostly. Bumps, scratches, that kind of thing. Like something moving around. Something you can't see."

Rhys was always the more thoughtful of the two. His parents sometimes told others that he liked his own space, as damning an indictment of social awkwardness as any. Though he and Steve were possessed of opposite characters, they had been friends since childhood, often labeled two sides of the same coin, but recently, they had been growing steadily apart. Rhys was growing tired of his oldest friend's bravado and misplaced machismo and was steadily phasing him out of his life. These days they met up only once or twice a month, but for old time's sake, they always tried to make it a night to remember.

Hence tonight's lock-in.

They had been drinking at a nearby pub when they bumped into a mutual acquaintance who told them about the recent happenings across the road at the Prince of Wales. They were skeptical, especially Steve, who suggested the stories were being fabricated in an attempt to boost trade at the ailing establishment. Never-the-less, intrigued and intoxicated, they set off to investigate. When they arrived, Steve wasted no time in confronting a fellow patron who was glad to point them in the direction of the proprietor. At first, the landlord, a chubby man who introduced himself as Les, seemed reluctant to talk about the disturbances, but a double JD and coke loosened his tongue.

"Apart from the strange sounds, is there anything else?" asked Steve.

"Oh yes!" Les the chubby landlord's eyes opened wide. "Things get moved around a lot. Little things, keys, money, my watch. Bloody annoying, that is. I took to hiding the important stuff, but the bloody thing always finds it. It turned into a kind of sick game, but I got tired of playing and moved in with my sister up the street. I don't appreciate all the graffiti art, either."

"Graffiti art?" asked Rhys, eager to make some kind of contribution.

"Yes, graffiti art. Has a habit of scratching things onto surfaces, does Jack. With a bloody screwdriver, it looks like!" Les the chubby landlord chuckled weakly.

"What are you talking about?" asked Steve. "Who's Jack?"

The landlord didn't answer for a while. Instead, his eyes switched from Steve to Rhys and back again. Finally, he let his head drop onto his chest. "Look," he began, a resigned expression creeping over his face. "If you two wanna stick around an hour or so, wait 'til all this lot has left, slip me a few quid in me pocket, like, and I'll show you."

Looking smug, Steve agreed for both of them, and they settled down at a corner table to wait it out. Egged on by the landlord's repeated calls of come on, you lot! Don't you 'ave 'omes to go to? the remaining customers gradually filtered out of the pub. By then Rhys was having second thoughts. Not because of any alleged ghostly activity, but just because he was getting tired and could think of a hundred things he would rather be doing than waiting in a pub for everyone else to leave. The landlord was probably taking a piss, anyway. However, he knew any attempt to leave the premises would be ridiculed by Steve. He could hear him now, speaking in that condescending way he used to manipulate people into doing what he wanted them to do.

You wanna what? Leave? What are you, chicken? Some kind of faggot?

Like most people, when his bravery was called into question it got Rhys' hackles up, and the mere prospect of it was enough to make him take evasive action. It was better to be safe than sorry, and just to go with the flow. To that end, it was he who jokingly suggested pooling their remaining resources to see if they had enough money left to bribe Les the chubby landlord into letting them stay the night. Steve, who may or may not have perceived the proposal as a challenge, readily agreed.

After the last of the late-night drinkers departed, Les joined them at their table. "You boys ready?" he asked. Rhys and Steve both nodded as one, and on his signal followed the landlord out of the lounge and into a narrow corridor.

"So how long has this all been going on?" Steve asked as they walked, obviously doing his best to extract as much pertinent information as he could.

"That's the funny thing, see," Les the chubby landlord began. "It only started when I came back from a family wedding in Ireland two months ago. While I was over there I did a bit of travelling and stayed at an old B & B outside Dublin. It was run by an old lady. I forget her name, but I remember while I was there, she kept talking about this character called Handsome Jack. At first, I thought it was another guest. Then I found out I was the only person staying there and thought she must be going a bit senile. She used to say Handsome Jack was acting up; hiding things, drawing on the furniture, making noises and that. In her head she thought it meant he was trying to get amorous with her."

"Same things that have been happening here..." Rhys added helpfully.

"Damn right," agreed Les firmly. "You know, I think it followed me back, somehow. Maybe I carried it back in my suitcase. Whatever it is, it came with me. Maybe it got bored over in Ireland and fancied a change," he offered another unconvincing nervous chuckle. For the first time, Rhys noted beads of sweat standing out on his forehead.

"Why did she call him Handsome Jack?" asked Steve, digging, digging.

"See for yourself..." the landlord said as he stopped and pointed at pointed at a section of plaster-coated wall.

Against the nicotine-stained surface of the wall, Rhys was surprised to see a vast array of deep scratches exposing the pink plaster beneath the paint. It was the color of cooked salmon. Most of the marks were indecipherable, but a few words stood out: PIG, WATCH, and FUCK. The most prominent word was repeated several times: JACK.

"Well, it looks like the name is right. But how do we know he's really handsome?" asked Steve, as if it mattered. Sometimes it was like he asked questions all the time as a result of some inner compulsion, some longing to be heard. A psychologist would have a field day inside his head.

Unperturbed, the landlord simply shrugged. "Dunno. It's just what the old lady in Ireland called him, and I'm not about to start calling him ugly, am I?"

"Guess not," Steve said. He gave Rhys one of his looks, then said, "We were thinking..."

"Go on," the landlord said, as a knowing look descended on his face as if he already knew what Steve was going to say, and he probably did.

"Would it be possible to stay here the night? Kind of a ghost hunter's vigil? We wouldn't be any trouble, and we'd pay you for the privilege, of course."

Les the chubby landlord's round face positively lit up. "And how much would you be willing to pay? For the privilege?"

"Twenty-two pounds seventy-two pence," replied Steve without hesitation, the total sum of their pooled resources.

***

"What was that?" Steve asked again of the scratching sound when his first question remained answer-less. "That noise. Did you hear it?"

"Hear it, are you crazy? It sounded like it was right here in the room with us," Rhys replied. He hopped nervously from foot to foot, anxiously looking about the sparse back room the landlord had permitted them to use and fighting to control the tendrils of panic that began to snake down his back like cold fingertips. His breath hung in clouds before his eyes. The temperature had dropped dramatically and quickly, but that wasn't all. The very atmosphere seemed to have changed. It was probably down to simple heightened emotions, but it could quite possibly be a result of something altogether darker and more malicious. The air was now super-charged. Something was going to happen, soon.

Without warning, the sound came again, even louder this time. Steve jumped out of the chair where he had been trying to remain calm, and both young men's heads whirled around. There was nothing to see, just empty space filled only by a tiny three-legged chair throwing suggestive shadows against the far wall.

Was the stool there before?

Rhys couldn't remember, but now it looked out of place, surreal, like a mini fugitive from war of the Worlds. It seemed to be quivering. He was about to mention this to Steve when suddenly, the stool lifted itself completely off the floor. It moved slowly at first, then gathered momentum as it was raised higher and higher by unseen hands. Then it was flung across the room with such tremendous force that it shattered against the far wall. Pieces of splintered wood dropped to the ground.

In that instant, every shred of bravado and embittered masculinity evaporated and both young men turned on their heels and made for the door. Rhys got there first, and flung the door wide, but before he could get his body through, he was brutally wrenched back by Steve, who used his superior size to wrestle Rhys out of the way and barge him aside. In the struggle, Rhys fell to the floor, but his friend didn't even hang around long enough to help him up. The door slammed shut, and to add insult to injury, from his prone position on the hard wood floor Rhys heard the jangle of keys in the lock. "No!" he screamed. Too late. The lock clicked into place, and after that it was only the sound of footsteps retreating at pace down the corridor.

***

Steve was awoken early next morning by the shrill tone of his mobile. Squinting against the invasive daylight and bolts of white-hot pain shooting through his head, he fumbled around until the handset fell into his grasp. Without looking at the display he hit the RECEIVE key. "Hello? Who's that?"

"Rhys. Just ringing to say I'm okay. Not that you care."

The voice on the other end of the phone sounded thick, and anger bubbled just beneath the surface. Remembering the events of the previous night, Steve's face flushed with shame. How could he just run off and leave his oldest friend alone like that? Even worse, he locked him in that room with whatever it was that threw the stool against the wall. "It wasn't like that," he was trying to justify his actions both to himself and the voice on the other end of the phone. "Not like that at all. Hey, what happened, anyway? After... after I left?"

"Nothing."

"Nothing?"

"Nothing. I just waited in the back room for Les the landlord to come and let me out in the morning."

"What about the noises? And the flying stool?"

"It was a cat," said the voice.

Steve frowned. There had been no cat. Why was his friend lying to him? What was more, his tone had changed. All traces of anger had left his voice. Now he sounded self-satisfied, even smug. What did he have to be smug about?

Something was wrong.

"... fancy it?"

His friend had been talking the whole time, the words washing over Steve's consciousness like a flood. "What did you say?" he asked, his heart beginning to thump in his chest.

"I said I downloaded the new Lostprophets album, if you wanna come over for a listen."

Steve glanced at the clock on his bedside table. It was just after 8am. The new Lostprophets album wasn't due to be released for a few days. Sure, an advance copy may have been leaked to the internet. That wouldn't be unusual. But Rhys would have dropped that in if that was the case. Besides, who invites people over to listen to music at this hour? Confused, Steve mumbled an agreement and hung up his handset. He felt woozy and numb. His mouth was dry and a raging thirst made talking, and even swallowing, difficult. He needed fluids.

He opened his bedroom door and made his way gingerly down the stairs. Bypassing the bathroom for now, he went straight to the kitchen to get a drink. It was cold in there.

His flesh was instantly peppered with goose bumps. As he stood at the sink filling a glass full of water from the tap he happened to glance at the worktop to his left, and what he saw there made his breath hitch in his throat.

Etched into the wooden surface with what must have been a knife or some other kind of sharp tool were two words: JACK'S HERE.

RICHARD THE VAMPIRE

by Joshua Malbin

Johsua Malbin holds an M.A. from the Johns Hopkins creative writing program and has taught there and at Deep Springs College in California. His stories have appeared in the *Beloit Fiction Journal*, the *Cimarron Review, Bitter Oleander, Juked*, the *Cream City Review, The Drum*, and the online editions of *n+1* and *Stymie. Richard the Vampire* is about money and class.

He'd been trying to get his memoir published for fifty years now. Back in the Sixties, a human editor at a sci-fi publishing house had urged him to write it. The man knew what he was and thought he could market the book as a novel.

Unfortunately, he'd had a lot of ground to cover and wasn't all that literate. He'd been nearly 200 before he'd learned to read and write, and he had all the same difficulties with it as anyone who'd been uneducated most of his life. Eventually, he sped things along by hiring a writer and dictating, but not long after he did his editor friend dropped dead of an aneurysm, probably related to his cocaine habit. No one else at the small sci-fi house wanted to continue the projects that editor had left behind. The vampire spent more money than he'd ever have thought possible on postage to send the typewritten manuscript to one publisher after another, and each time it came back in the big manila envelope he'd prepared and pre-stamped, he lost a little heart.

Twice now, in the years since it was first finished, he'd had to hire new writers to overhaul the thing, since even he could tell that the style had gone stale. Both times when they finished, he ate them.

It seemed to him that his book really should be drawing more attention by now. Novels about his kind sold quite well, so his story ought to be as appealing as Twilight or The Southern Vampire Mysteries, or whatever. He'd listened to parts of these on audiobook and thought his most recent writer matched up against them just fine.

He wasn't sure why he'd attached himself so persistently to the idea of publishing a book. It hadn't even been his idea in the first place, and he hadn't done the writing work to realize it. He supposed that after so many centuries of simple survival, he'd grown hungry for significance, the kind of hunger humans sated with family or religion. He wanted that experience of touching something more important than himself, and he thought he could get it if people read his history and loved him for it.

Or maybe he'd just fixated on it as something to accomplish in a long, otherwise dull existence.

****

One day, he saw online the photo of another novelist and recognized him as a vampire. He had written exactly the book Richard had been trying to sell for years, his own memoir passed off as fiction.

Richard knew him mostly by reputation, though they'd met three or four times over the years. He was an aristocrat who'd gone by various names over the years, and aristocratic vampires like him in any years had been no likelier to mix with common ones like Richard than mortal aristocrats had been to mix with commoner humans. They hadn't even come face to face until the late 19th century in America, when such a thing became conceivable. The aristocrat had expressed surprise at how old Richard was. He'd never known a vampire of base birth to last so long, he'd said. Gentlemen vampires could hide indoors for months, even years, without being bothered, but others tended to be found out and destroyed.

That was one major difference between their tales, anyway. The first centuries of Richard's story were about survival. He'd skulked in the wilds between villages and hidden in attics when he did come to town, held out against his hunger until it became unbearable, and then struck quickly and furtively. Meanwhile, the aristocrat had written about entertaining Mozart, Samuel Johnson, Moliere, and drinking from Marie Antoinette just before her beheading. Richard didn't know whether any of it was true —he doubted, for example, the anecdote about a four-way with Benjamin Franklin and two courtesans at Versailles— but even if the aristocrat had done none of what he'd claimed, he had been around those people and knew enough details about how they'd lived to make it all seem plausible.

****

The aristocrat had published his book under the utterly ridiculous single name of "Cain." Richard went to a reading of his at a bookstore downtown. He wasn't entirely sure why he went—no, that wasn't true, he knew why he was going. He wanted Cain to help him get a publisher, or at least an agent. He just wasn't sure he wanted to acknowledge that reason or act on it. It might not be shameful for someone of this century, since no one had shame about anything today, but for him, it meant begging a nobleman for help, abasing himself before a vampire who'd had everything he'd always wanted—peace, security, and food—and now taken this too.

On purpose he arrived late, five minutes after the event was scheduled to begin, and slipped into an open seat in back. These things never started strictly on time, and all around him humans were buzzing, meeting, feeling out their neighbors to see what use they could make of each other. Half the people here, it seemed, were trying to sell "dark fantasy" novels, to use their term. Being there for the same reason as everyone else only made Richard more ashamed.

A pretty young woman from the bookstore introduced herself and told them they could buy copies of this remarkable book after the reading, it was stacked by the registers near the exit. Then she read Cain's bio off a sheet of paper, and Richard was surprised to hear the real history of Cain's life, perhaps slightly embellished, rather than a made-up history of himself as a human author. Of course, she did read it with an ironic expression that implied they were all in on the joke, were merely going along with the conceit that the author was a vampire.

Then Cain took the podium. The last time Richard had crossed his path had been in Los Angeles in the 1950s, when he'd had his hair cropped close and wore a sport jacket and checked shirt like a beatnik. Here, he'd affected a preppie author look, growing his hair to his collar and wearing an unnecessarily bulky scarf.

He opened a copy of his book on the lectern and cracked the spine. "The Summer of 1816," he declaimed. "Lake Geneva. The Year Without a Summer, when it rained nonstop. Percy, Mary, George, John, and I were at the Villa Diodati, taking laudanum. We'd been doing it for three days. Mary was gorgeous, a delectable, languid, opiated creature whose veins pulsed slowly in the lamplight and firelight. I had been trying to break myself of the habit of falling in love with mortal women, especially young, married women, yet between us there was quickly growing a heat that could not be denied. More than heat: under the influence of the laudanum, I felt I could sense her great soul, all the immense potential the world and her dissipated poet of a husband had yet to see, and I wanted to experience that greatness as long and as deeply as she would allow it."

It went on like that. Cain was in love with Mary, who was pretty without being stereotypically beautiful. He loved her for her soul. He thought Mary could love him too. One scene where he caught her alone on the stairs went on for nearly five minutes of body language and significant looks, with little actual dialogue.

Eventually the fivesome, drugged out of their minds, decided to write each other ghost stories to pass the time. Cain didn't write anything, he said, but talked about the legend of vampires, what they were capable of doing, and so intrigued Mary that he managed to lure her to the kitchen and sip her blood. He described the puncture wounds he made on her neck as "delicate, barely noticeable, only deep enough to bring to the surface a few precious drops of her—through which I fancied I could taste a deep, powerful essence, a spirit that would soon change the world." He was so overcome by that essence, he claimed, that he restrained himself from drinking any more and rushed into the Swiss rain to feed on the first shepherd he encountered. When he returned, the others were reading to each other, Mary Shelley from the story that would become Frankenstein, and then George, Lord Byron, the fragment that would later be finished by John Polidori, his doctor and laudanum supplier, as The Vampyre, the first such story in English. He didn't say it outright, but Cain strongly implied he'd inspired both.

"Mister Cain—" ventured a slightly overweight, freckled young woman during the Q&A that followed.

"Just Cain is fine." Cain beamed her a smile so benevolent it verged on creepy.

"Ah." The woman gathered herself. "Yes. Ah, what would you say are the similarities between Byron's time and today? That is to say, ah, why were vampires so big then and why now?"

"Excellent question." The smile never wavered. "Over the years it's something I've had a great deal of time to think about, of course. I would say that vampires flourish when empires are tottering and about to fall, or when they've just fallen. You don't see them bubbling to the top of the popular imagination when a society is expanding, unafraid of anything. It's only when everything seems insecure, then people start looking for enemies among their own elites to explain why what used to be great is in danger of falling, and that's vampires. So after the fall of Napoleon, you get The Vampyre from the Continent, even if it sold in Britain, and in the waning days of Queen Victoria, you get Dracula. The Weimar Republic is responsible for Nosferatu. For a long while, perhaps, you Americans were only aware at the back of your minds that your empire was failing, and from that cultural subconscious came vampires, the shadowy elite powers that repel yet fascinate you. Now, of course, it's become so obvious what's happened to your empire that you have protests against elites occupying all your cities."

****

Afterward, Richard couldn't bring himself to go to the podium to have his book signed. Yet he still felt he needed to stay, because he'd come, shown himself, and gotten nothing. He helped the bookstore staff fold chairs and lean them in stacks against the wall, hoping that Cain would notice him and at the same time that he wouldn't.

He did. After the signing line was through and most other people had left, Cain and a few others remained in a knot at the front of the room, putting on their coats. All the chairs were folded, and Richard now merely stood uncomfortably by the door, pretending to scan the magazine rack. Cain looked straight at him, so it was clear he'd known Richard was there all along, and beckoned.

"We're going to a restaurant," he called. "Why don't you join us?"

If Richard had been capable of blushing, he would have.

****

They sat at the back of a tiny bistro, nearly a dozen of them around a single long table made of several smaller ones pushed together. All the way there, Richard had trailed the rest of the group, not sure how to engage any of them in conversation. When they arrived, though, Cain made a point to introduce him to everyone.

"Richard is a vampire too," he announced. Reactions were split. Half seemed entertained by the extension of Cain's gimmick, the other half tried to hide their annoyance at it. "I've known him for just around a century now."

"Do you have a memoir too?" asked a woman from the entertained half. She had the slightly overfed look of those whose career required professional lunches. Maybe an agent or a publicist.

Richard nodded. "It's pretty different from Cain's. We've led very different lives."

"You'll have to send it to me," the woman said but did not volunteer her name or mailing address before turning to the man sitting to her opposite side and striking up a conversation about some editor or other who'd just been fired. Richard didn't care. He could find those things out; he'd follow her home later if need be. No, this meant he'd done what he'd come for. He'd gotten a referral without humiliating himself. He could relax.

"Let me ask you something," he said to Cain three glasses of wine later. He'd begged off ordering food, claiming a "special diet," and the same half of the table had been amused. "What you said about empires, is that why you think your book sold now? Because I've been trying for a really long time."

Cain laughed. "No, that was bullshit. I just looked at all the books out and saw they're all about vampires in love with human girls, so I put in a bunch of that. Teen girl fantasy, Richard: an older sophisticated man who's also a pretty, protective, strong bad-boy type wants her more than anything, and he doesn't care about looks, unlike guys her own age. He appreciates the depth of her soul, that secret specialness that no one else in her life seems to understand. That's all it is."

****

Yet Richard remembered the Year Without a Summer. In 1815 he had been trailing Napoleon's reconstituted army, hoping for a return to the fat days when he could sneak onto battlefields after dark and feed on the wounded and dying. He'd eaten well during the Napoleonic campaigns. In fact, he'd eaten well for many years, going all the way back to the French Revolution. But there was no sustained return to these happy times. There was only the single feast of Waterloo, and then a few months later a bitter cold autumn. Clouds shut out the sun and dirty brown snow fell early, making it possible for him to go outside many days before dusk.

He'd headed south, for Italy, where he hoped it would be warmer. Not that the cold bothered him directly, of course, it was just that French peasants had an inconvenient habit of staying indoors and sleeping nearly all day during the winter, leaving him nothing to eat. He only made it as far as Zurich, though, before snow blocked the passes.

That was all right at first. He'd spent some time in Switzerland in the previous decade, when it had been a battlefield between France and Austria. The Swiss had been delicious. He thought he could wait there until spring, meanwhile feeding rarely as possible to avoid raising suspicions, sometimes even eating dogs he caught in the street.

Only spring never fully came. The temperature rose above freezing, yes, but clouds continued to block the sky, and cold rain fell endlessly, day after day, into May, into June. When the city expected farmers to bring their spring produce, few came and they had little to sell. Worse, they brought worry about the grain harvest, far more important than the fruits of their market gardens. The corn and wheat were rotting in the fields. The cold and rain had to stop soon. If it didn't ... it simply had to.

It didn't stop. It rained through July and August, a dreary, endless rain that turned the whole city into a single giant muck puddle, a cold soup of animal shit, human shit, drowned mice, and mud. It was good hunting again. No one investigated a corpse too closely when it was face down in that mire.

In late August and early September it became inescapable: the harvest had failed. Last year's grain and flour were running low and this year's wouldn't be nearly enough. Ten years of war had emptied all the stores that might have saved them. The price of bread rose to seven cents a pound and long lines formed outside bakeries before dawn. Richard would see them on his way home.

By December, there was no bread and people were starving. The canton government bought grain from Italy, and while some was stolen en route, much of it did arrive. It was far too little, though, as hungry country families had come streaming into the city, doubling and tripling the need. Churches made thin soup of whatever they could buy and hundreds of gaunt people fought over it.

There was an outbreak of typhus. Richard glutted himself on the dying, who tasted rancid.

Over the winter, they learned of a new prophetess traveling the countryside in the northwest, close to the Alsatian border, preaching about the duty of the rich to help the poor. At first, they heard her name, Barbara-Julie von Krüdener, only from the burghers' newspapers, which labeled her a socialist trying to incite the poor to riot. After a while, though, they began to hear good things about her too: she was a baroness who'd sold all her lands, rights, and jewelry to buy food for the poor. She set up soup kitchens wherever she went, preaching the love of Jesus Christ. In the spring of 1817, a pamphlet she'd written to the poor, the Gazette des Pauvres, arrived in Zurich, telling them that even though Satan had taken hold of the rich and induced them to neglect their duties of charity, Jesus had never forgotten them and would bless them doubly for all the injustice they suffered in life. The burghers' papers denounced her as a revolutionary, but the poor only loved her more and clung to her as their sole hope in a world falling apart.

When she herself came to Zurich in June, they packed the Lindenhof square to hear her and the canton government was petrified. Richard couldn't be there during the day when she preached, naturally, but when he got there at dusk, a massive crowd was still there waiting for her to reappear, or else perhaps waiting for a portion of soup. Thousands of hungry, desperate people, wearing the remnants of what had once been sturdy workingman's clothes, all now spindly and weak. They weren't so different from the masses of poor in the streets of Zurich every day, except they held themselves straighter, looked you in the eye and asked for nothing rather than crowding around and begging. Some had arranged themselves in family groups under the trees and rolled out what bedding they had, preparing for dark. Richard couldn't imagine that all of them had heard one woman standing on a table, or whatever they'd found to serve as a podium. Many must be there simply to be part of this community and be valued despite their poverty.

He envied them. Here they were, fallen from the social order and barely clinging to survival, and they'd found their self-respect and built a provisional new society. As someone who'd clung to survival for a hundred years, that whole time beneath normal social and economic life, he understood deeply how good it must be to find a place that respected and valued them even in their misery.

Yes, he envied them, and envying them hurt. When the fires in camp died, he thought, he'd tear through here like a wild dog. It had been a long time since he'd killed for any reason but hunger. These people made him itch for it.

He noticed, though, that gendarmes were forming ranks on the edge of the square nearest the river, at least two or three companies in full uniform, muskets standing up in rows like the pikes of their Guard ancestors. It was already dark enough that few people in the square noticed them. Richard did only because his night vision was sharp as any nocturnal hunter's. He was the only one to see them shouldering their muskets, too. They tried to aim over the crowd's head, but they couldn't see where they were shooting any better than the crowd could see them, and they weren't close to a precise formation.

At the first volley, some people in the encampment merely looked around, confused, while others—Richard guessed veterans who'd been following Frau von Krüdener awhile—began gathering their few belongings at once. Close to him, a young mother folded a pot, a spoon, and half a loaf of bread into one half of a blanket, then wrapped her year-old son in the other half so only his head stuck out, tying all of it into a single bundle. A man just beyond her set his rough clay bowl upside down on his head like a hat.

At the second volley, the crowd nearest the gendarmes broke and fled, smashing into chaos the ranks of their slower-reacting neighbors as they ran through them.

In the third volley, some gendarme's muzzle must have dipped too low, because under the tang of gunpowder, Richard smelled blood. He made his way toward it, starting and stopping, dodging sudden rushes of panicked people and then racing across open ground in the moments he found it clear. The gendarmes were no longer firing: now through roiling people and smoke he saw glimpses of them advancing with clubs or the butts of their muskets, forcing the crowd away bit by bit.

Then he located his victim, a middle-aged man shot in the back, high up. He wasn't dead, and groaned in pain when Richard slung him onto his shoulders. He carried the man to a nearby alley, deposited him behind a carriage house, tore off his shirt, and drank from his fresh wound.

****

So that had been 1816 and 1817. It had felt like civilization was falling apart, that there might never be enough food for the poor again, and that the revolutions of thirty years before would begin all over. Europe was tired of bleeding and tired of going hungry, and yet it seemed like it might never have peace and plenty again. Cain might claim he'd been bullshitting his audience, but he wasn't wrong, and he might even have been aware enough of the poor of 1816 to know it.

****

He stayed late at the restaurant, drinking wine with Cain long after his human entourage had left. With them gone, Cain could drop the pretense of pretending to be a vampire, and the two of them exchanged gossip of mutual acquaintances from a hundred years before. Richard grew drunk and sentimental. He told Cain they should make more of an effort to be close, since there were so few of their kind left. Cain agreed, but Richard couldn't tell if he was being sincere, and he knew that tomorrow he'd analyze his memory of the exchange carefully, trying to decide if he'd been groveling before the prince.

They emerged from the restaurant into a crisp fall night, just cool enough to make the air seem clean. A block away, policemen had massed, their uniformed backs all in a row, and from beyond them rose the rhythmic shouts of protesters enacting a People's Microphone. Together the cops and Occupiers blocked the way to the nearest subway. Richard and Cain turned away from them and headed uptown.

"Did you really have an affair with Mary Shelley?" Richard asked.

"No," Cain said. "I was there, I was the one who really brought the laudanum, but I could never get a taste for those straitlaced rich English women. Give me a fat peasant wife any day."

"But what do I do?" Richard demanded. "I never even knew anyone like that. Is that why no one wants to read my story? Because I'm not an aristocrat like you?"

"Probably. These are days of blue blood again," Cain told him. "But haven't you noticed that the more you strive for something, the less likely you are to get it? This isn't a

143

virtuous life, Richard, that rewards hard work and perseverance. That was a dream Americans had for a while, that they could become their betters, but they're waking up. You're one of those betters now, and you've been around too long to stay asleep."

****

On the news when he got home, Richard watched scenes of the clash between cops and protesters he and Cain had just avoided. There had been similar run-ins all over America that day, and even in Zurich, where Occupy Paradeplatz had been encamped at the heart of the Swiss banking industry, in that very same Lindenhof Square. One young man they interviewed spoke about the indomitable sense of community they'd forged in their encampment, a feeling of belonging to an important cause in a world whose elites had turned their back on them, and Richard saw the same fresh dignity he'd seen among the disciples of Frau von Krüdener two hundred years ago.

He hated that young man, and kept on hating him while he printed out a fresh version of his manuscript, prepared a cover letter, and stuffed both into a 10 X 13 envelope. Cain had given him that woman's name from dinner, and the internet had served up her address.

RESPONSIBILITY
by Paul Stansfield

Paul Stansfield was born and raised in New Jersey, and works as a field archaeologist. He has had stories published by *Bibliophilos*, *Morbid Curiosity*, *Generation X National Journal*, *Aoife's Kiss*, *Conceit*, and *InDTale*, among others. He currently has two eBooks available with Musa Publishing-- *Dead Reckoning* and *Kaishaku*.

Victor typed in the final sentence of the email message, chuckling as he did. It mostly concerned the Rod Stewart/soccer team story (urban myth?). He still couldn't believe that Cindy had never heard it. Just as he was about to send it to her, the screen hummed loudly, then went blank. All the lights on the keyboard were now off, too. What the? What was wrong with it? Victor waited a few seconds, and then hit Control/Alt/Delete, then the power button, then repeated both of these sequences again and again when nothing happened. He checked the power cord connections, but all of these appeared fine. Next he switched the plug into another outlet, one that was definitely working, in so far as a lamp running off of it was shining warmly. No change.

Well, that was it; he was fresh out of ideas. Damn computers; so mysterious and so frustrating. Victor went to his final solution. "Vomitus piece of goddamn shit!" he yelled. He was sorely tempted to slap the computer a few times. Its huge price stayed his hand, though. That was it. He'd have to call one of his computer smarty friends for the millionth time and try to have them talk him through the problem based on his confused, possibly incorrect explanations. Victor was reaching for the phone when he noticed a distinct chill in the room. Crap, was the heat broken too?

His hand touched the phone. Just then, he saw movement out of the corner of his eye. He turned and stared in surprise at the man standing in the middle of his living room.

"Esape Toretta Etoufremile Zen Frotavo!" the man said, as far as Victor could make out. "Yowila Pupunu Malamala Buliguo!" The speaker was dressed in what looked like furs, and he was rather short and squat. His beard was dark and wild.

The man grunted inarticulately for a few moments more (or was it more of his language? Victor didn't know), spat on the floor near Victor, and then disappeared.

Victor shook his head to clear it. He must be tired or something, he thought. His brain needed a rest from the computer screen, apparently. Thoughtfully he checked to make sure there was no spit on his carpet. It was clean. Old imagination took the ball and ran with it, he thought, it....

Four more men appeared, and one woman. The woman was in a ragged sack dress, and sported a nasty, dripping, head wound. She didn't match any of the other men, or they to each other. One was black, one was Asian, one was Middle Eastern, and one was Hispanic. They were all dressed in military apparel of various sorts; some just cloth, some leather, one in chainmail. The five strangers all spoke quickly, in turn. More nonsensical babble ensued for about a minute. Several punctuated their tirades with vicious arm gestures. Then, just like the first man, they disappeared.

Victor stared out into the room as the visitors left. The cold was still here, he realized, and if anything had gotten worse. He rubbed his arms and waited.

Seconds later more people were in his room. This time there were six of them. Various ethnicities, time periods, and injuries were once again represented. Victor didn't wait for them to speak.

"Who are you, and what do you want?"

They seemed to ignore him and go on with their jabbering, each in turn. The sixth one, though, a tall man in a simple tunic, whose intestines were spilling out onto the floor (or were they?) said something Victor could understand.

"I am Maurice. You killed me, Victor Sebastian Chulkhurst. I won't rest until you fully understand my pain."

Victor's response was interrupted by the man and his cohorts' disappearances. Then four more people blinked into being. Victor repeated his original question, and got the same lack of response. This time, however, as he listened more carefully he thought he could pick out his name again, although it was extremely accented and partially mispronounced.

During the next reappearance (five this time, two women, two men, and a child of indeterminate sex) he bypassed the questions for a few statements of his own.

"I don't know who you are, or how you know my name, but I haven't hurt or wronged any or you. I couldn't have, since you're strangers!"

The only difference this time was that one of the figures pushed his lamp off the table. It broke with a crash, and went out. As they blinked out Victor strode over and checked the wreckage. That was solid proof of them. Quickly he pulled the plug.

This time it was eight people. More yelling, and once more, what sounded like his name. The fourth one, a massive Indian looking guy, actually walked over to Victor, and before he could react, the intruder slapped his face roughly. Stunned, Victor lashed out at his assailant, only to punch futilely at the empty air. So, they're solid, eh, he thought. With that he sprang out into the center of the room and flew into a crowd. He felt more intense cold and an odd, heavy air sensation, but that was all. He turned and kicked at a man and saw his foot fly though the man's stomach. Seemingly nonplussed, the man screamed, "Killer. Providence will punish you!"

Victor ran for the phone and picked it up. He was greeted with silence. Suddenly, a woman with no teeth jumped right at his face. Surprised, Victor fell back, only to feel nothing substantial. He made a break for the front door. As he got within five feet he saw the bolt and chain draw themselves, and then something solid tripped him.

Defeated, he sat down on his floor and watched the parade of confrontation.

* * * * * *

Father Malcolm kicked at a dandelion on the grass strip right by the street, outside of his church. He watched as the dozens of little helicopter-borne seeds scattered across the turf, the sidewalk, and the street. He fidgeted agitatedly. What was Rabbi Saul's deal? Father Malcolm had always thought of the Rabbi as being a level headed fellow, but his phone call had been weird. Meet some very troubled young man outside of his church at two P.M. Why outside? And why couldn't Saul give him more detail? Curious, very curious.

A murmur caused him to shift his gaze up from the ground. Malcolm watched as a young man came around the corner. After a second, suddenly, a group of people came out of nowhere surrounding the man. They drew near him and yelled excitedly, each one in turn. Then, just as suddenly, they disappeared! Father Malcolm blinked and rubbed his eyes.

"Father Malcolm, I presume?" The young man had stopped about fifteen feet away. He was speaking loudly. A second later more people appeared and resumed screaming at him. As Malcolm watched, one threw a punch at the young man's chest. As it connected, the attacker and the others winked out.

Malcolm stumbled over his words. "Yes. You're..... Vic-Victor Chulkhurst, then." As he said the surname, more people appeared, once again a different group. They were dressed in odd, old fashioned clothing, like robes or armor. One was even wearing skins.

Victor sat down on the sidewalk, and motioned with his hand for Father Malcolm to do the same. "I asked Rabbi Saul to ask you to meet me outdoors so your church didn't get busted up. The first church I tried, as well as Rabbi Saul's synagogue, had stuff broken by my entourage here. As a word of warning, they might yell or strike at you while we talk. They try to interfere with everything I do. Although they haven't tried to really hurt anyone yet. But just so you know." This was all spoken over more shouts from the visitors. Father Malcolm was slightly disturbed by them and didn't respond for a few moments after the pause. He noticed there was a constant chill in the area surrounding Victor.

"I'll take that under advisement, Victor. Thanks for the warning, and your concern about my church. Who are these...ghosts, and what are they doing?"

Victor laughed slightly. Malcolm tore his gaze away from the blinking in and out people and really regarded the man for a moment. He was sandy haired, average height, and a little portly. Although it was a warmish day, he was wearing a winter jacket, obviously to combat the cold caused by the spirits. Victor was very tired looking, too, with big dark circles under his eyes. Actually, one of the dark circles looked like it was combined with a bruise.

"That's an excellent question, Father. I've been wondering that very thing and hoping you can help. Rabbi Saul mentioned you were...unorthodox in some ways. Specifically about getting rid of ghosts. He thought maybe you could help me."

"But," Father Malcolm watched as a young spirit covered in blood ran at him with a fierce face. As he shrank back he saw the girl get right up to him and disappear, and then a horrible chill ran through him. He whirled around in time to see his attacker reappear and then disappear behind him. "Sorry," he managed, "That's a little scary and distracting." Victor smiled tightly and nodded knowingly. "Anyway," he said, raising his voice over the din, "Like I started to say, I've cleaned houses of ghosts before, but not from an individual."

"I realize it's out of your usual territory. I was hoping it'd be close enough. You use prayers and invocations against them in houses, right? Won't they work on me? Anything." His voice took on a pleading tone.

"Well, there's what I used before. I can certainly try them on you." He shivered violently. Malcolm had felt cold spots around ghosts before, but none as bad or long lasting as this.

"Sorry about the chill. They suck energy or something. Please, Father, please give it a try. And I'd grab a coat while you're inside."

Father Malcolm nodded and turned away, and walked back to the church. As he got about fifty feet away, it was the normal temperature again. He stared back at Victor. Victor was still sitting on the sidewalk, the ever changing procession of ghosts surrounding him and yelling at him in turns. He sure was taking it calmly, Malcolm thought, or was he mistaking resignation for calm? Malcolm snapped out of his musings and walked inside his church. He passed through it to his living quarters attached to the back. They were simple; a bedroom, kitchen, bathroom, living room, and study. A few minutes of searching on his desk turned up what he needed. It was a slim book on exorcisms and driving out evil spirits, written by a Catholic, of course. His peers in the United Methodist Church didn't believe in such things. They believed in a metaphorical rather than tangible evil. Malcolm had seen and read enough things to convince him otherwise, so he'd acquired and used books like this one. The bishop overlooked this eccentricity in such an otherwise well liked, talented minister.

Malcolm also retrieved a vial of holy water, a larger crucifix, and his coat. Then it was time. He sighed and walked back through the church and out towards the tormented man. Despite his reputation, Malcolm had only cleansed a few houses, and these had been individual, rather shy ghosts. Nothing like what he faced here. He stood up straight as he approached Victor. Chin up, Malcolm, he thought, be a good religious warrior, help out this poor boy.

As he got to within fifteen feet of Victor, he noticed a face at a window of the house across the street. Just as quickly the person backed away, and the curtains were redrawn.

"How have other observers reacted to what's happening to you?" he asked over the clamor.

"Most do double takes, then take off themselves. Convinced they're hallucinating or sure that they're not, but are too scared to intervene. And the ghosts aren't afraid of an audience, either, as you can see. They don't care. You should have seen my landlord. My neighbors complained about the noise, of course. Plus the landlord was pissed about all the furniture destruction. But then she ran when she saw there were ghosts around."

"Furniture destruction, huh? They're breaking a lot?"

"Hell yes. My computer, my TV, my car, my DVD, my stereo, bed, chairs, everything. I gave up and started camping out in the national park yesterday. Luckily, it's warm enough. Good thing, since my sleeping bag is good up to negative twenty degrees, but can't withstand spirits ripping it apart. Not that I'm sleeping much, anyway."

"They don't ever give you a break?"

Victor's eyes looked hunted. "No. They haven't left since they appeared two nights ago. Exhaustion gets me to sleep over their yelling, but being shoved repeatedly wakes me up. I grab about fifteen seconds of sleep at a time." He paused. "That's why I'm here, mostly. I can't take much more of this."

"Speaking of which, I'll get started." Malcolm slipped closer to Victor, right up next to him. He opened his book and started reading aloud, asking God to dispel the obviously unhappy spirits that were afflicting Victor. Every so often he gestured with the crucifix, and he liberally scattered holy water around, both on Victor and the ghosts themselves.

The effect was very disappointing, to say the least. The situation didn't change one bit that Malcolm could see. Every few seconds came with a new barrage of ghosts, who each said their piece, then disappeared, only to be repeated endlessly. They took little notice of the minister, the prayer, or the holy water. A few spirits gave him a mad face, one or two jostled him to confront Victor better, but that was about it. Victor was still their main focus. Malcolm got to the end of the prayer and stopped. The previous three times, this one had been enough. The effect for those had been immediate and palpable. He and the house's occupants had instantly known that the ghosts had gone. Not so this time. Chagrined, he leafed through the tract and started another prayer.

The minutes rolled by, and dozens of series of ghosts flashed by. It was funny that way. Malcolm was still aware of the ghosts, but his fear was dwindling. They were becoming more irritating than frightening now.

Suddenly, a Neanderthal-looking ghost casually flicked Malcolm's prayer book out of his hands, and then shoved him to the ground. Malcolm held up his hands to defend against further blows. None came. His attacker and his comrades were gone and then replaced. Malcolm sighed and retrieved his book. As he did, he noted a Buick slowing down to stare at them, then it accelerated abruptly down the street.

More minutes went by. Father Malcolm finished the second prayer, and then a third. There was still no change. "I'm sorry, Victor. Normally the one prayer is sufficient. I'm not making a dent. I think there's too many."

The hunted eyes found the minister's, and then blazed into anger. "What? That's all you can do, Godboy? You were a big fat waste of time!" A cuff from a woman wearing a Renaissance era dress shut Victor up and knocked him down. During the next hiatus, Victor spoke again, this time in a more reasonable tone.

"Oh crap, I'm sorry, Father. It's just the strain, and the lack of sleep. I know you're doing your best."

"That's okay son. I understand." He paused and listened to one of the ghosts. The spirit's use of Latin had sparked Malcolm's interest. "Why is he accusing you of being his killer?"

"Yeah, others have said that, too. The few I can understand, anyway. That's what I'd like to know. I swear I've never killed anyone." Victor stopped and yelled right at one of the ghosts. "Hear that, assjack? You're all wrong! I never killed anybody! Piss off!" Then he turned back to the pastor. "Can you think of anyone who could possibly help me?"

"Let me think." Malcolm retreated back out of range of the ghosts. He noticed a man walking his dog down the street. As they approached, the dog barked and whined uncontrollably, and dragged its owner back the other way. About ten more cycles had passed when Malcolm remembered someone. "Oh," he exclaimed. Quickly, he whipped out his address book and recopied a name, address, and some basic directions onto a blank sheet. Then he ran over to Victor, timing the handoff for a ghost gap. "This guy, Simon, is a medium. The real deal. He owes me a favor. I'll call ahead and tell him you're coming. I don't know if he can do anything, but it's worth a try, I guess. I hope he's home."

"It sure is worth a shot. I'm willing to try anything." Victor stuffed the piece of paper into his pocket just as another ghost cycle began. During the next few hiatuses he committed the information to memory, knowing his tormentors would very likely rip up the piece of paper. He hesitated, plotting the best route in his head. This took some doing—he'd been spoiled by his Garmin over the past couple of years. Too bad Casper and friends had broken that too, he thought bitterly. He wanted the least traveled roads, so there'd be fewer chances of accidents from surprised observers.

"Victor. Have any of them attacked you seriously yet? Or has it just been the slapping around type of thing?"

"A couple of them attempted to beat me severely, and one even tried to throttle me. The others pulled him off. Luckily one of the peacemakers was an English speaker. She said, "No, don't. We all get a turn.""

"A turn, huh? Wonder what that means." Abruptly Malcolm stopped his idle thinking. "Sorry, Victor. I'll make that call. Good luck, son, and God bless."

"Thanks, Father. Later." Victor trudged off. He had a three or four mile walk ahead of him. The ghosts had trashed his car almost first thing. At least he was getting his exercise, he thought bitterly.

* * * * * *

Victor walked down the street, checking house numbers. It was coming up. Boy, what a neighborhood this Simon lived in, he thought. The hotlines must be extremely popular. The entire block was mansions, huge and complicated, with monstrous yards, all enclosed by gates or hedges. Finally, he reached 328 Pineview Terrace.

As he got near, a man stepped from behind the gatepost and smiled at him.

"Hello, Victor. And ghosts. Follow me." Victor trailed behind as Simon led him through the gates, which shut automatically after they were inside. The medium wove through a grove of trees until they reached a small clearing. Victor marveled at Simon's house as he walked. It was immense and looked a little like the White House. There were large columns and fierce gargoyles on the outside. An Olympic-sized pool and tennis courts could be seen off to the side. Some digs.

Simon motioned for Victor to sit on a blanket in the middle of the clearing. He himself sat on one about twenty feet away. "I hope you don't mind us staying out here. I heard your specters get a little violent, and I don't want my stuff broken."

"That's cool. I don't want anything broken, either. You're doing me a favor, after all." He paused. "Speaking of stuff, you have a great place. I didn't realize that reading palms was so lucrative."

Simon laughed. He was a short man, and kind of ferret-faced, but friendly looking, somehow. "It's not. I have no customers. The only readings I do for other people are for family and friends. No, various lotteries, sports betting, and stocks paid for all of this."

"What do you mean? I thought psychics couldn't benefit themselves like that. That's what I always heard, anyway."

The medium laughed, more heartily. He seemed less perturbed by the alternating screaming torrents of ghosts than Father Malcolm had been. He was quite serene, even when a ghost or two shoved him. Simon was using a loud tone of voice but not shouting over the constant fuss. "Yeah, fake psychics can't benefit themselves that way, because they can't actually see into the future at all. That's just their excuse. Well over ninety-nine percent of the so called psychics are bullshitters who use psychological clues and vagueness to tell people what they want to hear. Us real ones actually use our ability."

"So if you're all knowing, how come Father Malcolm had to call you? How come you didn't contact me?"

Simon loosed yet another peal of laughter. "You're a cynic, Victor. I like that." His face grew serious. "I can't see everything. It's kind of frustrating that way. It's hit or miss. Some stuff I see and some not. Like I couldn't warn my mom not to drive down that highway on that particular night, but I could see that the Colts would cover the spread. I use what I can. As for you, I did have a feeling of foreboding that last couple of days, but it wasn't anything specific. But, let's get started. I also can sometimes establish contact with ghosts mentally. I assume you want me to do that, and find out why they're haunting you."

"Please."

Simon nodded and closed his eyes. His breathing grew heavy. Victor waited expectantly. A good ten minutes passed. A Samoan looking guy babbled at him incoherently and kicked Victor in the gut. Another one, a conquistador, threw a pine branch into the psychic's face. It bounced off softly. Simon didn't budge.

Another fifteen minutes went by before Simon opened his eyes. He blinked several time and grinned reassuringly at Victor. "I got in," he said, "That's the advantage of there being so many. Some didn't want to communicate with me, but some did. Anyway, it's real bad news, I'm afraid." His face fell. "You're the direct and only living descendant of the guy who invented the knife, like thousands of years ago, when they were still made of stone. All the ghosts you're seeing are people who were killed by knives. They think it's your fault."

"What?" Victor's scream outclassed the ghosts. "You're telling me that over thousands of years all these people were killed by knives, wielded by other people, long before me, and it's my fault because my great-great-great-great-etc. grandfather developed a weapon? My being born was a sin to them?"

"Hey, I'm with you. I think they're idiots. It's clearly not your fault, but they don't agree."

"And why now? Why didn't they haunt my birth parents, or their parents, all of them, before they died? Why me, why now?"

"Well, that's the funny part." Victor's face registered no signs of amusement. "Sorry, not funny for you, now, but there were some complicated twists in your family tree over the centuries. Orphans, adoptions, divorces, paternity issues. It took a lot to sort out. They only found out your lineage recently. They were haunting the wrong lady, actually."

"What? How absurd is this? So not only is my haunting unfair, but they did it to someone else who wasn't even the true relative?" He turned to a ghost and tried to strangle it. His hands, predictably, closed into air. "You're not even doing your homework, assholes. It's not my fault, anyway. You can't help who your ancestors were. I suppose all of your relatives were saints and never did anything wrong! And what's up with the knife thing, anyway? Knives are tools as well as weapons! The fact that some bad people use them to hurt people is that person's fault, not the device's inventor." He bellowed inarticulately. "If it wasn't a knife it could have been a club, or an arrow, or a bullet, or a sword!" Victor's head drooped toward the ground. The tirade had taken a lot out of him. Only his living audience looked impressed by his ranting. Gradually Victor calmed down. "Okay, Simon, what do they want? An apology?"

"They won't accept one, I'm afraid. Also, this may not be the time, but some of these ghosts were killed by swords. They consider it to be just a big knife. Plus, some were suicides."

"You gotta be kidding me…. Wait a second! Knives are pretty simple technology. Surely more than one person invented them over the years, over the entire world. So why haunt just me?"

"Yeah, I brought that up, too. They sort of admitted that, but said that it was your relative who was actually the very first one, so they're pinning it all on him. I know, I know, that's stupid, but that's what they think."

Victor just growled and muttered under his breath for a moment. Again, he got control of himself. "So what are they going to do, Simon? Kill me?"

"Ultimately, I think so, but you have to remember the sheer volume of spirits we're talking about. Everyone wants a shot at haunting you in turn. The ones who haven't gone yet won't let the others kill you before they get a chance, and at their current rate, it'd take lifetimes for all of them to reveal themselves. So what will likely happen is you'll be driven mad, die from exhaustion, or kill yourself."

Victor face buried itself in his hands, before a ghost ripped them apart, rubbed a bloody wound on his face, and then disappeared. "How come they didn't tell me all of this, anyway?"

"They thought it'd be better punishment if you didn't know; more mysterious and all. At least many of them did, obviously a few communicated to me. I guess none of the English speakers wanted to clue you in."

"And that's another thing. These fuckers have been around for a thousand years, want desperately to haunt me, and then can't take the time to learn a few words in another language. Lazy asses!" He spat at one of the ghosts (a samurai). The glob went through the target and landed on the grass. Victor faced Simon once more. "So what can I do, man? The ministers didn't work. Being in public didn't work. Crossing flowing water didn't work. Nothing worked!"

Simon stared back, and then he too bent his head, thinking. A kick to his shoulder was ignored. Abruptly he stood up. "Wait here, Vic. I've got something at the house that might help. Be back in a bit." He left the clearing.

Victor stood up and began to pace. Shit, he was screwed. He figured he was only a couple of more days away from a breakdown. He couldn't think straight. He'd avoided telling his family and friends because he didn't want to worry them (and they couldn't help him). He guessed he'd have to tell them now and hope no heart attacks would be caused. Some pressure in his bladder made him stop. Oh, good. Grinning for the first time in a while, he unzipped and took out his penis, "This is what I think of you, fuckers!" Spitefully he began to urinate on the ghosts. He walked about, getting each one. "Why don't you sons of bitches go into the damn light already? While you're there, you could, I don't know, bug the ACTUAL PERSON WHO KILLED YOU!" Victor finished and zipped up, then resumed pacing. The ghosts were unfazed by his excretory insult and his verbal taunts. They continued to appear, to yell at him, occasionally abuse him slightly, and then disappear.

A rustling in the trees caught Victor's attention. He turned toward the noise. Just as the spirits winked out, Simon was right next to him, and seconds later Victor felt agonizing pain in his abdomen. As he looked down, he saw Simon pulling a hunting knife from his belly.

Victor collapsed as though boneless. Blood flowed freely from his injured stomach. He looked up at the psychic in bewilderment. "Why, Simon? Why are you doing their work for them?" God it hurt.

Simon just stared down at him, a small grin on his face. He waited a good thirty seconds, then he bent down and tended to Victor's wound by pressing a thick towel over the cut. Victor started to struggle against Simon, but the pain was too much.

"Before you think bad of me, Vic, look around. Where are your friends?"

Victor managed to open his eyes, and turn his head back and forth. No ghosts. No yelling. The relative silence was refreshing.

"I gambled that this was the only way to get rid of them." Simon smiled slyly. "Plus, I had a psychic insight that I'd help solve your problem, so it was good odds. You're a victim of your ancestor now, too."

"Great," Victor returned softly. "You're like a doctor who chops the head off of someone with a brain tumor. Your cure was as bad as the disease."

"Oh bullshit. I called an ambulance before I left the house. They'll be here in a jiff. And I made sure I didn't hit your spinal cord, or something else vital. Medical science will heal you up. It's a bad enough wound to count for the ghosts, but not bad enough to kill you. You'll live. I know."

"You're quite the martyr then. I'll visit you in prison."

"You'll do no such thing. This was a freak accident, and you'll testify as such, if need be. You're my buddy who was checking out my new hunting knife, and you tripped and fell on it while I was holding it. No charges against your psychic friend. Or, if things still get threatening, I'll call on my high priced lawyers." An ambulance siren could be heard in the distance. It began to move closer.

"One more thing, Vic. As your advisor, I highly recommend against you having any children."

Victor looked at Simon and giggled briefly.

"Understood. I'll get a vasectomy as soon as I'm able. And thanks a million."

"You're welcome." Simon grinned back. The sirens were very close now. He ran back toward the gate, screaming, "Over here, over here."

Shortly thereafter, the ambulance technicians were ferrying their patient to the hospital. They were both a little confused. They had never seen a person take a serious stabbing so well.

THE BENEFITS OF BEING DEAD

by Benjamin Blake

Benjamin Blake was born in a small NZ town in the July of '85, and after spending time in Southern California and Australia, now leads a relatively reclusive life in the New Zealand countryside. His fiction and poetry has been published online, and in print, in Australia, the UK, and the States. His debut poetry collection, *A Prayer for Late October*, is now available.

Prologue: In the Vast Hands of the Ocean
Frankie Abraham's lungs were burning; his breaths came in painful, wheezing gasps. With each exasperating step, his oversized belly and thighs wobbled like Jell-O. His sneakers slapped against the wet sand, and he had to take extreme care not to trip over his left shoelace that had come untied. He didn't stop to retie it. He couldn't stop. The Gods that watch out over geeky fat boys hadn't granted him that liberty.

"Hey, Faggot! We're gonna stick a harpoon in your blubbery side, you gross piece of shit!' Ace Carrington shouted from somewhere a little too close behind.

Frankie was running for what could possibly be his life - at least for his physical and mental wellbeing. Ace Carrington and his two vicious buddies, Bruce Fanning and Lester Charles, had had it in for him for as long he could remember. As far as Frankie knew, he had been born and raised battered and bruised in garbage cans, and had grown up bloodied up and broken, in a sorry pile at the back of the football field. He was a loser. A total fucking loser. He had no friends apart from his little corgi, Sprinkles, he was terribly overweight, had to wear thick-lensed and even thicker rimmed glasses, and to top it all off, he was Jewish.

"What's the hurry, Kike? You see a bagel up ahead?" Frankie thought that had been Lester, his voice was higher pitched than the other boys'.

Unfortunately for him, and luckily for them, the beach was deserted. The only witnesses to the God-awful scenario were the crying gulls and the waves that crashed unforgivingly against the shoreline. And he was running out of beach.

The large, grey rocks that started once the sand ended were growing in size through his tear stained vision. He would have to stop once he reached them, and then take whatever beating was coming to him; just another day in the life of a fat Jewish kid; nothing out of the ordinary, nothing unexpected, nothing to get worried about.

"You're gonna have to stop running sometime, fatso! Need to save energy to suck your big-nosed daddy's circumcised cock later today!"

Frankie reached the rocks, and without thinking clambered atop of them. They were slippery from the sea's salt spray, and he had to scramble with his hands and feet to make any type of distance.

"Time to give up the ghost, Frankie, come on down from those rocks and take what's coming to you," Ace sneered.

Frankie didn't respond, he just choked back another sob. Ace and his buddies started gathering the smaller rocks and began to biff them at him.

"Stone the Jew! Stone the Jew!"

The rocks clacked against the ones surrounding him. He was trying to reach a large slab of concrete that was jutting out ahead. If he could make it to that, he thought, he could take cover on the other side till they went away; or decided to come after him.

A rock hit him squarely in the back; Frankie let out a small cry, and continued to crawl towards the slim chance of safety.

He reached the slab without managing to get struck too many times. His hand had taken a good hit though, breaking the skin, and blood was beginning to slowly seep from the fresh wound. Frankie sucked a deep breath of courage into his lungs and tentatively got to his feet. He took hold of the slab's jagged ridge and hauled himself up, scratching his stomach painfully in the process. But he had made it. Thank God.

"Don't you think you're getting away fatty fatty Frankie!" Ace screamed, picking up a rock. He swung back his arm, and pitched it with all his baseball-acquired skill.

Frankie felt the rock slam into his temple, causing a flash of blinding white pain to sear though his skull, and then he just felt dizzy. Dizzy, with the warm sensation of blood flowing down the left side of his face. His eyelids started to flicker shut.

He felt himself wobble, and then he tumbled into the furious hands of the ocean.

One: A Body is Laid to Rest, a Future Faux Par is Corrected, and Frankie gets a Peek of Something Worth Peering in a Window For Attending one's own funeral is a funny experience. Funny as in weird, or strange, and more than a just a little bit.

Frankie Abraham hovered near the ceiling of the synagogue, looking down at the pall-covered casket that contained his body. He found it hard to believe that in the belly of that wooden box, his recently departed flesh laid silent, bloated, and stiff, clad in his yarmulke and talit.

His body had been discovered washed up on shore shortly after the 'incident', by a man who was taking his dog for a run along the beach. That was yesterday. He still wasn't used to the afterlife, if this was even it. Well, it kind of had to be, didn't it; he was, after all, dead.

He didn't seem to be able to actually feel his body, it wasn't palpable, but it was still there, in a hazy, transparent kind of way. Come to think of it, it was pretty much the classic imagining of a ghost; the image of a person, but see-through and slightly shimmery. He was able to float about, as well as walk or run around the same as when he was living. The floating took a little bit of getting used to, but he thought he had mastered it pretty well considering that he had only been dead a little under twenty-four hours.

Frankie looked down upon the miserable congregation. He could see his father comforting his mother as she sobbed endlessly. He had been an only child, so there were no mourning brothers or sisters. Everybody else he didn't care much for. He had never really gotten along well with his aunts or uncles, or the few family friends that had felt obliged to attend.

As his casket was lifted by a solemn procession, he decided to get out of there. It was depressing. But where would he go? What was it one was supposed to do once they were dead? There should be a guidebook, or something.

He ascended through the ceiling of the synagogue and into the summer air. It was a nice day; the weather was a lot better than it had been on the morning of his death. Did the dead get deathday parties, the equivalent to the birthday party of the living? He didn't think so. Besides, who was there to come? His kitten that had gotten mowed down by an ice-cream truck when he was five years old? Was he supposed to go out and haunt people? Move into a nice rundown house and wait until a young family discovered it at just the right price? No, that didn't make sense. What purpose would that serve?

While Frankie was sailing over the houses of suburban Eavestown, he was struck by how stupid he was. The answer was painfully simple. Maybe the habit of not being one to take action in life was a little hard to shake now that he had crossed over. Maybe that's why the thought took so long to pop into his head, but he was glad it had. Frankie smiled as he dodged a confused gull. It was so simple. So very simple. One little word: Revenge.

But first, he had something to take care of.

The something Frankie had to take care of was a certain stack of magazines hidden under his bed: Playboy, Penthouse, and Hustler, among other titles, and some with slightly more questionable content, like the one with the schoolgirls and whips.

He had come across them while he was cleaning out the basement one spring. His mom had promised him ten dollars to help her out with the house and yard. Who the magazines had once belonged to, he had no idea. He just knew that he had never seen a member of the opposite sex naked before, and that wasn't something he wanted to prolong any further. Plus, it made the whole process of having a quick release a lot faster, and that was a good thing. Less chance of getting caught. That's the last thing anyone wants. How were you supposed to explain yourself when caught red handed with your pants around your ankles, tugging furiously on your schlong? He had averted the embarrassment in life, and he sure didn't want to face it in death. Plus, his poor parents had enough to be upset over without discovering that their son was a little pervert.

Frankie made his descent into the backyard of what was once his home and walked up the porch steps toward the ranch slider. He figured he probably could have just floated though a wall or something, but what difference did it make?

He walked through the door (literally, walked through the door) and paused as Sprinkles came running up to him, yapping and wagging her stub of a tail like crazy. So animals could see him. That wasn't surprising. He had read enough ghost stories as a kid, and the dogs always knew.

'Good girl,' he said, reaching a hand out to pat her head. It went straight through her.

'Damn,' he cursed.

She didn't seem to mind, though, and just stood there with a silly look on her face. 'Come on girl, let's go sort out this little problem about the porno mags.'

Both dog and boy bounded up the stairs and down the hall to his room.

It was exactly as he had left it before he had gone out for a walk along the beach the day before. He thanked his lucky stars that Sprinkles had been in one of her lazy moods, and had refused to leave the couch. Who knew what would have happened to her? Even if she had raised her hackles and bared her little fangs, an angry corgi didn't hold much of a threat.

Frankie sunk to his hands and knees, and shuffled under the bed. The magazines were hidden behind a couple of old Vans shoeboxes.

He went to shift the first box aside, and his hand passed straight through it. Of course, he thought, I'm not getting any brighter am I? A stupid fat boy, once dead, just becomes a stupid fat ghost.

He stood up, enough of the pretense; he didn't have to crawl about on his goddamn hands and knees like a retard. He glanced down; only the top half of him was visible above the unmade bed. It looked kind of funny. Like somebody had severed him in two and plopped his torso on the sheets. He hung his head in defeat and floated over to Sprinkles to say goodbye. He blew her a kiss, and then floated toward the closed window. Sprinkles let out a yelp, sounding like she was in pain.

He twisted in midair so he was facing her. She looked sad. Frankie felt a sudden fury engulf him. Thanks to Ace and his goddamn cronies, he was dead. He couldn't ever pet his dog again, couldn't ever stop by the bakery with his dad, or comfort his mom when she was upset, like she would certainly be when she found those magazines. Her only son was a fat, dead, sexual deviant.

He let out a cry of anguish, and felt a strange feeling surge through his body. Almost like he had stuck his hand in an open wall socket and had gotten a nasty shock. Sprinkles started yapping madly, and the rage grew. A fluttering sound came from the bed and the stack of pornos came skidding out from beneath, their pages flapping in a frenzy. "Wow," he thought, "maybe I'm not totally useless after all."

He focused his thoughts on the magazines, conjuring up images of them being anywhere else but his bedroom. The stack floated into the air, in small spasmodic movements. Okay, so how to get them out of the house? He twisted back around to face the window, and concentrated on it opening. He heard the magazines fall to the ground behind him - but the window had started to slide open. "So I can't do two things at once, okay, no big deal."

Once the window was open wide enough for the magazines to float through, he thought of his mother discovering a slew of pornographic magazines scattered across her son's bedroom floor, then breaking down in a sobbing pile on his bed. The magazines took flight again, a little more fluently this time. He raised a hand and made a gesture toward the open window. The floating plethora of porn followed obediently. The Playboys and Penthouses fluttered out of his room and out into the backyard. He then gestured towards his neighbors' yard, and the magazines soared over the fence. He smiled to himself; it was one of the strangest things imaginable. Flying pussy. The magazines settled on a table on his neighbor's back porch. The old guy next door would have some explaining to do to his wife, that was for sure.

***

The sun was beginning to sink in the west, casting Eavestown in the warm glow of early evening.

Frankie was heading toward Acorn Avenue, where Bruce Fanning resided, several blocks from his parents' house. He hadn't known this was where he had lived beforehand, but found, when he thought about scaring the asshole to death, that he had somehow known where to go. This was another pleasant surprise, just one more thing to add to the list of newfound post-life abilities.

He figured that maybe Lester or Ace lived closer, but he wanted to start with the less satisfying quarry and save the best till last.

On a street below, a light flickered on in an upstairs room. He realized that the house belonged to Susie Woodson, a girl who was in the same grade as him in high school, and subsequently, a girl whom he had had a crush on for several years. She also was frequently picked on by the same boys that had caused his death; they would throw things at her in class and call her names like "Susie-Slutface" and "Weirdo-Woodson." It had always made Frankie upset - she was a nice girl; she kept to herself and didn't fall into the superficial group of girls, who both dressed and acted like real life versions of Barbie dolls. She didn't deserve any harm.

He felt a small stab of guilt as he descended toward the upstairs room, though he would be lying if he said he wasn't at least a little bit excited. Still, was it wrong? Reaping revenge on Ace and his buddies was totally justified. But playing peeping tom to a sweet girl like Susie? Oh, well. What one doesn't know doesn't hurt them.

He sailed closer to the window, hoping like crazy that it wasn't going to be her parents' bedroom and he would catch an eyeful of something that he really didn't want to see. Risks were risks, and fortune favors the bold, or so they say, whoever 'they' were.

A lace curtain was pulled partway across the window, but a good portion was left uncovered. Frankie hovered in front of the pane and peered through. He was in luck. It was Susie's room - judging by the band and movie posters on the wall, anyway. He recognized the messy-haired singer of The Cure staring back at him from one, and remembered Susie wearing one of their tee-shirts to school on several occasions.

A moment later, Susie herself appeared, pulling off a white tank top, leaving her in just black panties and a bra. Frankie couldn't believe his luck. Being dead was fucking awesome.

Susie reached a hand behind her back, and unclasped her bra. Then, holding the cups over her pert breasts, walked over to the window and pulled the curtain. She had been so close Frankie had thought he had even been able to smell her, though he wasn't sure if perhaps that had only been a byproduct of fantasy.

Through the lace curtain, Frankie could see Susie's slim silhouette cast aside her bra onto the floor. He had come this far, he might as well go a little further, he thought, and began to concentrate on the curtain. It slid back to where it had been before Susie had pulled it shut. She was bent over, with the closet door open, pulling off her panties. "Wow," Frankie thought, "maybe I am in heaven after all."

She took a tee-shirt from a wire hanger, turned, and slid it over her head. Frankie let himself savor the image. Susie trotted over to the bed and picked up a pair of purple pajama pants. Then, she looked up at the window and screamed.

Frankie shot up into the dusk and away over the houses below. Had she seem him, or did she just get an awful fright from realizing that the curtain had opened itself? If that was the case, Frankie thought she had overreacted a little, but he had a feeling that wasn't it.

People hadn't been able to see him before; he knew that, otherwise his funeral would have turned out a little more interesting. When he had entered the synagogue, he had floated down the aisle like a phantom groom, and if he was visible, somebody surely would have noticed. However, he had opened the curtain. Maybe when he interfered with the land of the living, he was more solid, maybe the power it took to move things around manifested somehow. If that was the case, he had to be careful. He didn't think anybody that was actually living could harm him, but then again, what if somebody called a catholic priest or something - someone who knew how to perform an exorcism, what would happen then? He didn't know, and he definitely wasn't willing to find out. As much as Frankie wanted to execute his plan of revenge, he needed to do a little experimenting first.

***

Frankie scoured the streets for a fitting situation to prove his theory. Unfortunately, they lay quite empty. Direct action seemed like the best plan. The sooner he figured this thing out, the better.

He glided down into an area of town that he was relatively unfamiliar with, and chose a house at random. It was a white, two-storied home, with a light on downstairs.

Frankie entered the home of P.D & J.A Croswell (according to the letter box, anyway) via the front wall, and found himself in the living room. Large pictures of horses hung framed upon the walls, and an elderly couple was sitting on a couch in front of the television, watching a news channel. Frankie walked directly across their line of vision, and they didn't even flinch.

He then looked around for something suitable to gain their attention. He settled on a vase of dried flowers that was sitting on the dresser next to him. He envisioned the vase sliding off the dresser and shattering on the wooden floor below.

The vase inched toward the edge of the dresser and fell to the floor, breaking on impact. P.D and J.A Croswell jumped about a mile high off the couch and turned to face Frankie. He stood next to the broken porcelain, with his hands held out in a gesture that said: 'what the heck, these things just happen sometimes'.

The female half of the couple let out a small gasp, her eyelids fluttered, and then she fainted. Well, he hoped she had only fainted. The male half just stood there with a stupid expression on his wrinkled face.

Okay, so his theory had been proven correct. Frankie gave a polite wave and exited via the living room ceiling.

He felt a little bit guilty for scaring an innocent elderly couple, but in a way, it needed to be done, if not to them, then to somebody else. He had gained the priceless knowledge that he had to be a little bit cautious when using his "abilities". On the plus side, it would make dealing out supernatural justice to Ace, Bruce and Lester that much more satisfying. They would recognize him, they would recoil in terror, and most importantly, they would know why.

He resumed toward Acorn Ave in high spirits, swooping and somersaulting in the summer air. They would get theirs. Oh, yes, they would.

Two: The Cathartic Effects of Fire

Bruce Fanning's home was a decrepit thing; the lawn was in dire need of a mow, and the front gutter was hanging uselessly from the roof. A naked bulb was visible through the curtain-less windows. A garage sat to the side of the house with a light on. Frankie figured Bruce's dad was probably messing around in there.

Frankie floated through the front door. A terribly skinny woman was bent over the stove in the kitchen, cooking something in a large pot. Frankie didn't know what was cooking, but it sure smelt awful. An unshaven man was slumped on the couch in the living room, slurping a can of Pabst Blue Ribbon and smoking a cigarette. He tilted his back his head and polished off what remained of the beer.

"Goddamnit! I'm outta fuckin' beer, Angie! I told ya we should'a picked up another six-pack from the goddamn store. Fuckin' know I'm always right."

Frankie didn't feel any pity for Bruce Fanning - having a horrible family was no excuse for the things he had done to him. Frankie didn't pick on people just because he was fat, so why should a person make another's life miserable just because their parents were white trash?

A toilet flushed somewhere toward the rear of the house, and a moment later Bruce came moping into the living room.

"I'm going back out to the shed to paint my BMX some more."

"Yeah, okay, Bruce, just don't take too long, your mom'll have dinner ready soon, or she should do the useless bitch."

"I fuckin' heard that Stu! Maybe you should try cooking for once, you lazy sonofabitch!"

"Oh, shut the fuck up, Angie! I don't give a flying fuck!"

Bruce moped back out of the living room. Frankie followed. This works well, he thought. Bruce will be all alone, painting his little BMX.

Bruce opened the garage door and walked over to a work bench. His bike was in the corner, and as far as Frankie could tell, it hadn't been painted for quite some time. so then what was the asshole up to?

Bruce bent down and picked a can of gas up from the concrete floor. He lifted it with both hands, putting it on the bench and unscrewing the cap. He then stooped over it and put his face to the opening.

So that's what he was doing. Huffing gas. Frankie should have guessed that much.

Bruce took several deep breaths, sucking the toxic fumes deep into his lungs.

"Whoooooah," he moaned, grabbing onto the bench for support.

Frankie looked around for something that would be suitable to take care of Bruce. Empty beer cans; no, a pile of greasy rags; no, an empty Coke bottle; no, a Zippo lighter... yes.

A surge of sickening excitement flooded through him. Would he really do it? Could he really do it? God knew that Bruce deserved it. Anyway, what was worse? Taking care of a low-life scum bag, or letting him live to carry on in his malevolent ways for the rest of his life? What said that

Frankie was his first and last victim? Nothing did. Nothing at all. So it was settled.

It was time for Bruce Fanning to dine on what he dished out.

The gas can crashed to the ground, causing Bruce to cry out in surprise. "Motherfucker! Fuckin' thing. Fuck, I'm in the shit now. It's all over my fuckin' clothes! Dad'll beat my fuckin' ass!" Then the light bulb shattered. Bruce reeled around, "What the fuck?"

He started hyperventilating when he saw who stood before him, but it wasn't possible, he was dead. Bruce let out a giggle. "What a fuckin' trip! Shit, I don't think I'm gonna huff anymore gas. Just close my eyes 'till it goes away. Just a bad trip, that's all."

Something moved on the bench behind him, he heard a small snap, followed by a short scraping sound. "Oh, no fuckin' way! What the fuck, what the fuck?"

His Zippo was floating in mid-air, its orange flame dancing wickedly in the low-lit garage. He twisted back to face Frankie.

"Make it stop, make it stop, man, please, make it stop. It was Ace, man, it was all Ace's idea, I just did what he told me, I swear to God. Please, man!"

The dead boy smiled, and slowly shook his head. The lighter dropped to the floor. The spilt gasoline erupted with a loud whooosh, enveloping Bruce in its warm embrace. He screamed as the flames spread across his body, as they licked at his face and hands.

Frankie soared into the summer night sky, until the garage was just a small orange dot below.

It felt better than he had even expected. No remorse whatsoever, only a sense of uncanny peace, like something was a little more right with the world. One down, two to go. One dead bully, and a thousand fat and pimply kids across the country rejoice!

Frankie was filled with a feeling that was foreign to him: a sense of purpose. He would set things straight, one bully at a time. He was the phantom hand of post-life justice. He was the spirit of the night that would make the world a better place.

Maybe that's why he hadn't passed on to Heaven, or to Hell. Maybe it was part of the plan all along. Maybe it was his destiny....

Three: Video Games & Ferris Wheels
Stars burned bright in the sky, strewn across a dark canvas of night. A faint breeze blew though Frankie as he flew across Eavestown, and it felt strangely pleasant. His destination was the home of Lester Charles.

It was definitely a nicer looking house than where Bruce Fanning (up until very recently) had resided. It was a white, two-storied home, hidden behind a tall evergreen hedge. No lights were on throughout the house, but an upstairs room was faintly glowing. The colors seemed to be constantly changing. They went from red, to blue, to white, to red again. Frankie guessed it was probably the television.

Easy, Frankie thought. His parents are either asleep or, out for the evening. He knew that Lester was home, due to what he was now thinking of as his "internal tracking device" or should it be his 'infernal tracking device.'

He sailed up to the window and passed through the frame and panes. Lester sat on his bed, a video game console controller clutched in his hands.

"Yeah, got you, bitch!" He smirked.

Oh, no, I think I have got you, Lester old pal.

Frankie floated over Lester and hung in the space behind him. He was playing some type of shoot 'em up, taking out aliens with a spray of bullets. Frankie concentrated on the buttons of the console moving in the opposite of which Lester was pushing. His gun ceased firing, and he started to reload the weapon.

"Fucker!" Lester shouted, "I didn't tell you do that!" He frantically started hammering on the buttons. An alien being was approaching rapidly, closing in for the kill. It reached Lester's character and lashed out at him with a clawed hand. The TV suddenly went black and the words GAME OVER flashed across the screen.

"Fuuuuck!" Lester screamed, "I didn't fucking do that! Fucking piece of shit fucking game!" He threw the controller at the screen, and cursed once more.

The controller fought back. It jerked up off the ground and floated toward Lester. He just sat there, dumb and silent. The controller circled around his head, looping the black cord around his neck. Frankie gave a sudden jerk with his hand, and the cord tightened. Lester scrabbled at his neck with his hands. A low choke broke from his throat. Frankie came down in front of Lester, a grin upon his pallid face. Lester's mouth dropped open and for a second he stopped the panicked scratching.

"Game Over, Lester."

The cord around his throat tightened and he tried to loosen its death-like grip with trembling fingers. His eyes bulged in the sockets of his skull, and his face began to turn a deep red. He struggled in vain to suck even the tiniest breath into his lungs. He began to thrash and kick violently. Then, after a small, but satisfying amount of time, his body slumped, and stayed still.

***

Frankie celebrated the second name being crossed off his list by visiting Eavestown Amusement Park, which was situated beside the ocean. Not too far actually, from where his body had been washed up. He had loved going there as a child. He held fond memories of the smell of cotton candy, the joy of holding on tightly to the horse's neck as he spun around the merry-go-round, and of hurtling along the twisting tracks of the ghost train.

The park sat empty, forlorn and cloaked in shadows. Frankie passed through the padlocked gate and floated into the midst of the park, the lights and rides jumping to life as he passed. The giant Ferris wheel creaked into motion, the rollercoaster thundered along its tracks, an evil cackle escaped from the haunted house that the ghost train shot around in. Frankie smiled. It was a pretty sight. He wished he could enjoy it with somebody like Susie, though. He had never been granted that privilege in life. Who knew, maybe someday he would find another like himself, somebody he could wander the desolate suburban streets and empty amusement parks alongside. He stood and watched the merry-go-round for a while, reminiscing his lost childhood.

Somewhere, he heard a door open, followed by the thud of boots approaching. He turned and saw a heavy-set black man running toward him, holding a small handgun.

"Stop right there, asshole!" he shouted.

Frankie turned and walked into the night, ignoring the guard's threats of unnecessary violence.

Four: The Atlantic Welcomes an Unwilling Sacrifice

Ace Carrington lived in an affluent area of Eavestown situated on the west side of town that overlooked the ocean. His house was perched on the edge of a cliff; a rambling old thing with shuttered windows and several stories. A frayed American flag flapped in the night air, high atop its white painted pole.

Frankie felt a slight pull from somewhere near the top of the house. The evening was getting on, so he guessed that everyone had gone to bed. From what Frankie had heard, the Carrington family was considerably large. He wasn't one hundred percent on how many siblings Ace had, but it certainly had to be a few.

He entered the house through the outside wall and found himself in a bedroom. A little girl was asleep in a bed, snoring gently. He passed through the partway closed door, and entered a hallway. The pull came again, this time from above. He ascended toward the ceiling and passed through into what he guessed was the attic. Only it didn't look like a typical attic. A TV sat at one end, alongside the biggest stereo Frankie had ever seen, and the walls were adorned with posters of semi-naked women. An assortment of items lay scattered across the carpeted floor: Dirty laundry, magazines, worn out sneakers, an ice-hockey stick, CD's, schoolbooks, and videogames, among other things. A large, circular window was set in the west wall, the moon's light cutting through the dusty pane. A bunk bed was in one corner, but only one body was sleeping in it. Ace.

Frankie floated over to the side of the bed, and looked down upon Ace. He stirred in his sleep and muttered something incoherent. Frankie smiled as his covers ruffled back.

"Wake up, Ace, it's your birthday!" he whispered.

174

"Huh? Whataboutit? Wha? Go 'way."

"It's your birthday, Ace! It's your birthday! Wake up, wake up!"

Ace sat up and rubbed his eyes with his fists. "Huh?" They widened with recognition, his bottom lip trembled and he shot back against the wall.

"Okay, okay. So I was maybe lying just a little bit. It's not your birthday we're celebrating tonight." Frankie said, "It's your deathday! So come on, let's party!" Frankie reached a hand out to Ace. "Come on, buddy, what's with the messing around? The festivities await!"

The cotton sheet that was crumpled beneath Ace started to grow a darker shade, slowly spreading away from him. Frankie could already smell the acrid scent of urine. "Aw, somebody's a little too excited, aren't they?"

"Leave me alone..." Ace whimpered, on the verge of tears.

"Sorry, Ace. Not happening. What, you think after all that you put me through, the constant teasing, prodding, poking, kicking, shoving, name calling - and I could go on all night, that I would just leave you be? Everything you ever did to me in life just fuels the fire in death. Truth is, I don't think I can leave you alone, the pull's too strong. I have the strength to fight back now, and it burns through my essence like an inferno sent from the very depths of Hell. You messed up man, and it's time to reap what you sowed."

***

Ace Carrington was torn from his piss-stained bed and into the air. He tried, and failed, to stop what the dead boy was doing to him. His attempts were in vain. He was suspended in the middle of his attic room, the ghost boy hovering in front of him. He was smiling.

"Let's go for a little joy flight, buddy," he said, swooping through the closed window that overlooked the Atlantic. Ace felt something jerk his body into action, and like being pulled by an invisible rope, he followed. The circular window shattered as Ace's flailing body burst through it and flew out high above the ocean.

Frankie finally stopped when the shoreline had become but a series of twinkling streetlights on the distant shoreline. Ace was weeping, tears rolling off his face and falling into the ocean's swell far below, little droplets joining the much larger body of salt water. Apart from his screams, he had been silent. What could he say? Sorry?

"So this is it, Ace. Curtains."

The boy replied with another cry of anguish.

"But first, a little goodbye present." Frankie closed his eyes, and his face screwed up in concentration.

A long and tortured scream tore from Ace's lungs as every bone in his body simultaneously shattered. Then, he fell, still screaming, into the ocean.

Post Script: A New Dawn for Eavestown

The morning sun rose in the east, spilling its warm insides over Eavestown. Birds sang in the trees, and squirrels scurried about in search for acorns.

As the light of a new day poured in through her window, Susie Woodson got dressed, enjoying its warmth on her bare skin. She had dismissed what she had seen the previous evening to a slip of the mind, a by-product of an overactive imagination. She pulled on her favorite The Cure tee-shirt, and smiled.

It was going to be a lovely day.

THE PRICE OF RICE

by Mark Slade

Mark Slade has appeared in *Tales Of The Undead*, *Suffer Eternal 1-3*, *Hell Whore 2* and *3*, *Blood Moon Rising*, *Diabolic Tales III*, and *Tortured Soul 1* and *2*. He lives in Williamsburg, VA with his wife and daughter.

The bell attached to the door of Morty Hopper's shop rang. He heard the door screech to a close and bounce a few times before finding a resting place. Morty poked his head around the corner. He was in Aisle one, stacking baby food. At first, he didn't see anyone. He blamed the pair of glasses the new optometrist had given him. The glasses always made Marty's vision a little blurry. Then he saw a young woman materialize in front of the canned beats display.

She was fair haired and wore a purple scarf on her head. She was very pale, and she wore a tattered coat over a black dress that was ready to unravel at any moment. She stood there and looked around, confused.

Morty sighed. He didn't like being interrupted. He put an empty box in a trolley and rolled it out of his way. He fixed a kind and loving smile underneath his handle bar mustache.

"Good morning," Morty said in a sweet saccharine voice. "What can I do for you, Miss?" Morty towered over the young woman, and in his apron, white shirt, and tie, he hoped he sent a message to his customers that were a part of the authority in the neighborhood.

The young woman tried to speak, but stopped each time she opened her mouth. She seemed embarrassed. She looked away, smiled. A hand touched the scarf she wore.

"It's all right," Morty lied to her. "Take your time. No one is rushing you." Spit it out, will you? Morty thought.

'I'm sorry," She bit her lower lip. "I just live down the street--"

"Tumbler Ave. Yes?"

She nodded. "I left my wallet at home. My husband is with my baby. I was wondering if you minded giving me some rice on credit?"

Morty looked her up and down. That smile was wiped clean from his face. What does she think the kind of business I run? This is not a charity?

"I will come back and pay when I get home. It's just ... my husband will be angry with me. We haven't been ... getting along well since the baby ..."

A moment of clarity, or someone whispered in Morty's ears. The smile, half-hearted though it may have been, returned to his face. He held up his hand. "We may be able to work something out, if you promise to come back before I close at seven.

"I can give a few groceries." He couldn't believe he said that. Even old Mrs. Gaynes, a loyal customer, couldn't get credit. He realized he felt sorry for the young woman.

"Oh ... thank you," the young woman bounced a little. "I promise."

Morty took a pen and paper from his register. 'Just give me your name and address."

"Rachel Sommers. 11th and Tumbler. Apartment 12 C," She told him.

"Okay. Just go get what you need, I will ring it up, staple it to this paper, you sign it. When you come back this evening and pay it, you get the paper and receipt. Okay?"

"Yes! Thank you," Rachel said.

Morty waved a hand. "Go right ahead. Get what you need."

Nervously, Rachel looked around, took hold of a hand basket, and placed a loaf of bread in it.

Morty went to his office to get a cup of coffee.

As he was coming out of his office and back in the shop, he heard the bell again. Morty went to the register and didn't see Rachel at all. He walked the shop, peeking through five aisles until he came to the last aisle containing products for vehicles and detergents. There he had a fright. Mr. Klein was looking at the dish liquid.

Morty dropped his mug, the coffee splashed on his nice black shoes, the mug split in three large shards of porcelain.

"You scared the life out of me," Morty shouted. He bent down, picked up the pieces of his mug.

"I'm sorry," Mr. Klein shrugged his shoulders. "I thought you heard me come in." He went back to staring at four types of dish liquid.

"No, no. I was helping a young woman and she must have left without her receipt ...

Did you see her?"

"Huh? No." Mr. Klein said. 'I didn't see anyone. You got that new citrus burst? My wife loves the smell of it," Mr. Klein flashed one of the scariest smiles Morty had ever seen on a person still alive. "Mrs. Klein gets frisky after doing the dishes."

"I'm afraid I don't carry it. You sure you—"

"No. I'm afraid your store was empty, Morty."

Morty nodded to Mr. Klein, took the broken mug, and dumped it in the trash can by the register. "I guess she'll be back," Morty thought. "After all, we had a deal."

Seven p.m. came. Rachel was a no show. Morty was very angry. After he locked up, he pulled the fence around his shop so hard; the fence almost jumped the tracks. Morty put the chain and lock on, turned to the cold night and cursed everyone in the city.

Morty went home to an empty house, a Pomeranian, and the memory of Debra, his wife, gone ten years ago. He ate his frozen TV dinner and fed his Pomeranian two day old cherry pie. The TV was on an old police show from the 70s when Morty finally fell asleep.

He awoke the next day to begin the grind of selling fruits and Soap opera digest to the women of the neighborhood.

For two days, Morty waited to see if Rachel would return. At times he was sad she didn't come back, other times he wanted to find her and cause her a lot of trouble, whatever that would be. Morty wished she would have came back, settled the bill, so he could help her some more. There were days Morty thought of having a daughter. He often daydreamed about a past that never was. Putting her on the bus, walking with her to the pier. Watching her graduate high school and putting this imaginary daughter through college, only for her to drop out to get married and bring her son to his house.

Alas ... it was not to be in the real world.

The bell sounded. The door to his shop screeched shut. Morty was alert with hope it was Rachel at his door.

It was Manning, the neighborhood beat cop.

"Morty!" The short stocky man in ruffle blue uniform bellowed. 'Got any of those mint chocolates my Anna loves?"

"Karl," Morty sighed. He had known Manning since he was a little boy. His father had sold Morty all of the vehicles until his death. His mother was a beautiful red head in her day, of course Morty never told Manning that.

"Well, don't be so happy to see me, Morty."

"I just thought you were somebody else." Morty said.

"I'm sure I'm your only customer today."

Morty gave a half smile. "No. I was hoping someone come back and settle a bill."

"Oh yeah? Was she a young woman, blond hair?" Manning looked through the candy rack, found what he he was looking for, and gave celebratory ho-ray.

Morty was stunned. "How'd you know?"

"Old man Grumman had the same incident, and so did Tyler in his store on 23rd. A young woman comes in, asks for help for food. Says she left her wallet at home, hubby will be mad if she don't come back with something. Weird thing, she always asks for rice and its only thing missing. Right?

"You know ... I never really checked. I thought that basket was another customer's ... come to mention it," Morty thought a minute. "Yeah. I think rice was the only thing missing."

"Tyler even went to the address this lady gave--"

"Her name was Rachel. Rachel Sommers." Morty blurted out.

Manning lifted an eyebrow and looked funny at Morty. "Yeah. That's the name he said. Anyways," Manning shook his head and laughed. "Tyler went to the address ... get this ... she ain't there. It's a black couple that answers the door. So she's scamming all of you old shopkeepers and food vendors for fuckin' rice! Ain't that something?"

Morty was thinking, but Manning took it the wrong way. He thought Morty was disgusted with his foul language.

"Yeah, yeah, Morty. I'm sorry about the cursin' and all. I'm goin'. See you later," Manning threw down three bucks and left.

Morty picked up the money and opened the register automatically. He closed the register, still lost in thought.

"Something's not right," He said to himself. He went to his office and poured himself a cup of coffee. He stood in the baby aisle, took a sip. Then he remembered.

Morty had read a few months back in the local paper about urban legends, local legends of townspeople long gone. Some were from the Revolutionary war. Some were from the nineteen thirties. The one that has now come to light is a tale of a young woman begging shop keepers for a handful of rice, which first surfaced in the early nineteen sixties.

When one shop keeper refused the young woman, he was found dead and bloated in his store with rice trickling from his gaping mouth.

When Morty read about it, he didn't believe it, but now that he has seen Rachel, if that's her name, he has no choice but to believe in the legend. While she was in the store, a customer had not seen her presence. Nothing terrible has happened to him or other shop keepers because they complied. She received her rice.

"Remarkable," Morty said. Morty thought of the other stores near him. There is a fourth store, Morty thought. Simms. Dan Simms store on Beaker, about a block from Morty's. "I wonder if Rachel has been there?"

Morty rushed around to close up early. In less than five minutes, he had turned the lights off, locked the door, and locked the fence. He was out beating the pavement toward Simms' store.

When he arrived at Simms' store, Simms was lying on the floor between the card rack and the candy aisle, rice trickling out of his gaping mouth.

Morty stumbled out of the shop door, trying very hard to keep his composure. He wandered away from the building in a stunned haze when he caught a glimpse of Rachel. She was walking toward a wooded area past a playground.

Morty followed her. He even called out her name. She didn't respond. Nor did she turn around. She ended up at an old oak tree that never seemed to sprout leaves, at least as long as Morty could remember.

Rachel vanished. She was no more.

Morty went to the oak tree, touched it's cold dead bark. He walked around it several times, hoping Rachel would reappear. On the third time around, Morty noticed the bottom of the tree trunk was liquid now.

He stooped as low as his old back would let him. In that milky liquid was a child, a new born, very pale, but not thin. No, if it were not deathly white, he would think that fat little bugger was healthy. But it's skin was barely hanging on. And when the baby opened it's large black eyes, that was when Morty tried to run.

The baby hissed, exposing tiny sharp teeth and a forked tongue. It reached out of it's milky womb in the bottom of the tree and pulled Morty inside.

The bell to Morty's shop sounded off. Officer Manning appeared and walked past Rachel. He tipped his hat at her. "Morning Ma'am," He said. He saw Morty behind the register, just staring at nothing. Manning stared at him a few minutes. Then he spoke. "Yo, Morty, got any of that chocolate raspberries my Anna loves?"

Morty smiled drearily. He nodded and pointed to the candy rack.

Manning turned, his back to Morty, and went to the candy rack. "What? Cat got your tongue Morty?"

Morty came up behind him slowly, stiffly. He felt weighed down. Hard to move around. Especially when he had a baby attached to the right side of his midsection.

"You could say that," Morty told Manning.

www.ingramcontent.com/pod-product-compliance
Lightning Source LLC
Chambersburg PA
CBHW051511260626
47162CB00008B/2925

* 9 7 8 1 6 2 0 0 6 2 8 5 2 *